MW00788409

A Robin's Snow

2017

Diana –
Very nice meeting you!
Enjoy –
Barbara Briggs Ward

BARBARA BRIGGS WARD

A Robin's Snow

Copyright © 2017 Barbara Briggs Ward. All rights reserved. No part of this book may be reproduced or retransmitted in any form or by any means without the written permission of the publisher.

Published by Wheatmark®
2030 East Speedway Boulevard, Suite 106
Tucson, Arizona 85719 USA
www.wheatmark.com

ISBN: 978-1-62787-487-8 (paperback)
ISBN: 978-1-62787-488-5 (ebook)
LCCN: 2017900641

Book cover designed by graphic artist Lisa Hainline.
For more information: lisahainline.com

The snow kept falling—the wind kept howling in that split second—a second that forever changed the life of Annie Finley

Growing Up

ANNIE KNEW BY THE TIME SHE turned twelve that it was Daniel Finley she would marry.

The two had been in the same one-room school through the eighth grade. It was with Daniel that Annie walked the mile and a half every day alongside the winding road that slipped out of view once past the elder's place. At first he was just the quiet boy who lived on the farm beyond the plank bridge stretching over the creek. But over the years, this shy boy evolved into a strapping young man—handsome, sure, and infatuated with the little girl who'd blossomed into a strikingly beautiful young woman. In required Amish tradition, Daniel Finley asked Annie's father permission to marry her when she was just shy of nineteen. There was no hesitation. They married the next fall following the harvest.

8 years later

ALTHOUGH STILL DARK, ANNIE COULD TELL there was a fresh cover of snow outside. It was a connection she had with the fields she and Daniel worked. Every season the earth demanded their attention, as did their son Jacob and the quilts Annie made and sold for quite a hefty price. It was a full life for Annie and Daniel Finley. Although born into simplicity and those boundaries, Annie remained as free in spirit as the lingering spits of snow now circling the cornstalks left standing in the November wind.

It was a sudden gust blowing a window wide open that drew Annie's attention to the far corner of the bedroom. Jumping out from under the blankets, Annie secured the latch. A hint of the new day would soon etch itself into the horizon. Annie found early morning soulful in ways she could never explain. But she didn't have to. Daniel understood. He respected Annie's independence. It was part of why he loved her so. He knew she kept magazines hidden beneath old floor boards in the barn. He'd seen the tubes of lipstick in her dresser drawer; enjoyed the times she'd wear the lipstick to bed.

Another strong blast blew the window wide open again. Papers scattered, whipping about the bedroom with its loft ceiling. Annie hurried. She didn't want Jacob to awaken yet. They'd returned home rather late from a full day with family. Today would prove even busier. With her sister exchanging wedding vows in a few hours, there were still last minute details that needed tending especially in the kitchen. She'd told her mother and siblings they'd be back before dawn. Annie had mixed feelings about this union. She felt her sister was settling. She knew Mary didn't love Ira. How could she? At least seventeen years her elder, he'd been married. He'd had thirteen children with a woman who keeled over one sticky August afternoon while canning beans. Short, stout, his scruffy beard was often peppered with bits of food stuck to it like glue. The only time his pipe wasn't hanging from the corner of his mouth was when he was eating. Annie wondered about the men dressed in black suits stopping by to talk with Ira in his barn. They never smiled when speaking. They'd only stay for a few minutes, then speed off down the gravel road as if in a hurry to get somewhere. But where Annie wondered? Annie tried talking to her elder sister—one of five elder sisters—but Mary always walked away.

"We all can't marry a Daniel Finley," was Mary's usual reply.

That was at least the truth thought Annie as the north wind tossed her long down-to-the-waist licorice hair around her face, covering her chocolate eyes and full lips. Reaching up to brush her hair back, Annie's hand was met with Daniel's. In one swift move, the window was back in place. The latch was fastened tighter than bark to birch trees scattered about their acreage. Without saying a word, Daniel scooped Annie up in his arms and carried her back to their bed. They made love as if this was their wedding day.

Preparations

BESIDES THE HALF-EATEN BOWL OF HOT cereal he left on the table, Jacob hadn't taken many bites of the warm bread covered in strawberry preserve sitting on a plate in front of him. It was his favorite. Annie worried he might be getting sick. She watched as he tried looking out the window for his father but it was still dark outside and Jacob was still half asleep. Scratching out wiggly designs on the frosted panes with his fingernails, he never noticed how heavy the snow was coming down. Late fall always brought some snow. It'd mix in with colorful leaves making for breathtaking landscapes. But this Tuesday morning Annie didn't appreciate the white cover. They were in a hurry. The thought that Jacob might be falling ill bothered her.

Using a few layers of linen, Annie covered the cooled cracker pudding made earlier; then cleaned up the kitchen and tended to Jacob. Daniel was finishing his chores. He'd soon be back inside to get ready. With about four miles to go, Annie made sure Jacob dressed warmly. Noticing the top button of his overcoat was loose, she took a moment to sew it back in place. As she did, Jacob came over, holding his favorite blanket and the book they'd been reading before bedtime. Last night there'd been no time.

"Tonight, Jacob. When we return we will read."

Annie picked her little boy up. She'd made the blanket before he was born. He still took it to bed with him. Throughout her pregnancy, Annie sensed she was bearing a son. Over 9 pounds he was and breach, with slight sprigs of hair and eyebrows faintly outlined. It'd been a hard birth. So hard that despite what midwives kept telling him, Daniel sensed Annie and the baby were in danger. That's why he made her as comfortable as possible in the buggy and reassuring her all along the way, brought her to the area hospital. Doctors told Daniel he'd made the right decision. The baby might not have survived if he hadn't.

"We must leave our baby in God's hands Annie," said Daniel as he'd hurried the horses. "It is God's will that we must trust."

Needless to say, they felt truly blessed when they were able to hold their newborn perfect in every way. Annie remembered kissing his little fingers thinking he might play piano or write a great novel when he grew up. Annie didn't think in terms of what was expected. She preferred to think in terms of the unexpected. Jacob's love of books pleased her. He'd ask questions. He'd express opinions that for a youngster not even five, were quite visionary.

"He's a fast learner," Annie would tell Daniel. "He's able to understand both worlds."

Annie made it clear to Daniel that Jacob must be made aware of his surroundings. This was kept between the two of them. Annie realized that as Jacob grew the world around him would be even harder to resist. Should he decide to leave, she wanted their child prepared.

Annie was thankful for the two women who'd stopped a few summers back. They noticed Annie's quilts hanging on the clothesline. The women were from the city. Their business was discovering Amish craftsmanship. They'd resell the goods to high-end shops and boutiques around the country. Annie's quilts were sought after items, fetching a fair price. They were in catalogs. They were featured items online. Even *Sundance* had hopped on the marketing bandwagon. Through these women Annie was able to get Jacob all kinds of books. They were also Annie's source for magazines and newspapers.

"We love finding books for Jacob," they would tell Annie. They always came with a box full.

Annie took a closer look at her child now sitting beside her. She'd decided awhile back he'd be quite tall. The spitting image of Daniel, his blonde hair would probably turn as had Daniel's. Annie felt Jacob had a gift for music. That was why both flute and harmonica were part of their nightly routine. They kept this a secret. Instruments were forbidden.

Annie's mother was constantly after her to fetch another child.

"You're getting old Annie. It's time again to bear the fruit of your husband. You must submit to his will. It is your duty as his wife."

Little did her mother know that submitting as she described the act of making love was a constant, although Annie's definition of submitting was much deeper than merely laying back as her mother did whenever Annie's father decreed submission.

Annie decided she needed some sort of control over the size of their family.

"It never made sense to me to keep pumping babies out one right after another even if it was proclaimed a duty. Most of the time growing up my mother never called me by my right name. She had so many children. We became one generic brand, blending into a single mass of never-ending chores," she'd often say to Daniel, himself from a family of eleven. There had been twelve but a brother out plowing a field had been dragged to his death by a frightened horse. She and Daniel talked about children at great length. They took nothing for granted, feeling truly blessed with Jacob. They decided it would be right for them to practice a natural birth control. And so, going against the foundation on which their beliefs were cemented, Annie Finley, a young Amish woman of individual mind and spirit, kept track of her cycle with a calendar hidden underneath her stockings in a dresser drawer.

The Arrival

ALTHOUGH THE HOME OF ANNIE'S PARENTS had been rearranged to accommodate benches for seating attending guests, there were other items that still needed tending. As organizer, Annie would be sure to bring her lists. She'd crossed off her sister's wedding gown. Mary made her dress, a deep shade of navy, months earlier. She'd done the same for her two attendants. Younger sister Hanna and her intended beau Ezra had been published the same day as Mary and Ira. They would be married next week. But today Hanna and their cousin Elizabeth would stand up for Mary. Annie paid no attention who Ira had chosen. She'd assumed it would be two of his six sons.

"I think we're ready," said Annie, helping Jacob with his boots while taking one last look around the home Daniel and others had built. Perfectly located—far back off the main road, the house faced directly into sunsets Annie felt were painted just for them. Trickling through the back field was a brook that, in springtime, stretched beyond its banks. All about were thickets with rambling grapevines and clumps of wildflowers. A forest of pine and maple made a natural boundary as did Annie's huge garden spreading from near the front porch all the way down and over to the birch trees.

"Bring Jacob's blanket Annie," yelled Daniel walking down the front steps with the pudding in hand. Guided by lingering stars and a kerosene lamp attached to the side of the carriage, Daniel led the horse out of the barn. The snow had stopped but Daniel knew anything could happen as winter was nearing.

Hurrying into the front room, Annie found the blanket along with the book she'd promised to read later. She placed it on the kitchen table. That's when Annie remembered Jacob's stuffed bear he'd named Bear sitting up on his bed. She'd been going to make him another plush—a bigger one—but her quilts demanded her attention. Maybe for his birthday thought Annie as down the stairs she came. Turning off the lamp, Annie checked Jacob's scarf, tucking it further down around his neck.

"Look what I have my little one!" Annie held out Bear.

Just by Jacob's reaction Annie was glad she'd decided to bring the worn toy along. If he were to get sick, he'd have his favorite things. Picking Jacob up, Annie opened the door, turning back around for one more look. She was already anticipating returning home.

It wasn't as cold as Daniel had predicted even after getting on the main road where the wind was more apt to bother them. Daniel brought extra blankets and with Annie holding on to Jacob, the three were quite comfortable.

"I have an awful feeling about this marriage Daniel. I can't explain it but something isn't right."

"I should think it's because of Ira's thirteen children. Don't let it ruin your day. Look Annie. Jacob's sound asleep."

Annie brushed aside the few strands of hair teasing Jacob's forehead, then pulled his blanket closer to his face, shielding him all the more.

"We are lucky Daniel. We are so very lucky."

Nothing else was said as the horse led them along the paved highway. Turning onto a gravel road, they began noticing other lanterns swaying ahead of them. A thin line of buggies with a common destination had formed without anyone orchestrating the parade. Some would stay through the last meal. Others would stay for awhile and then leave for yet another wedding. This is a most fertile time of the year for the community thought Annie as Daniel pulled back on the reins and jumped down off the buggy. That's all it took to awaken Jacob, now rested and ready to play with cousins—so many cousins.

The Wedding

ALTHOUGH JUST APPROACHING 4:30 THE HOUSE was wide awake with excitement. Much of the food prep had been done, including the making of over 400 doughnuts and all sorts of cookies. Ira had finished chopping off the heads of thirty-five chickens and, as tradition, Mary and Ira had washed the celery. Food preparation would take place in the summer kitchen due to the anticipated number of guests. Along with benches, tables would be set up in the main kitchen as well as the front room after the vows were taken. Meals would be in shifts.

Annie preferred the summer kitchen. It was much smaller, with a ceiling at an angle and windows overlooking her parents' endless acreage. While Daniel waited in the barn with the other men, Annie tended to matters at hand. The bride, groom and their four attendants would soon be fed, then change into their wedding clothes. Annie decided when it came time to serving Ira she'd leave that up to one of her cousins. Looking down her list Annie double checked the four couples assigned as roast cooks who'd divided up the dressed chickens and taken the foul home to cook. Potatoes still needed peeling. Cole slaw still needed to be made. Annie's mother would prepare the roast. Although she followed the traditional recipe, no one could mix the shredded chicken and bread like that woman. Her arms were as bulky as any man's.

Dawn was etching its way into the day like a window shade slowly rising. Annie looked about for Jacob. She found him with other young-sters under the care of older cousins gathered on the front veranda, watching unhitched horses being led to the barn by the chosen Hostlers. Annie felt certain that when Jacob reached the age of fourteen he'd be chosen as a Hostler. He had a sense about him.

"He has your disposition," Daniel frequently remarked. "Jacob is as stubborn as his mother."

Annie's list was getting shorter. With Mary upstairs dressing, Hannah raced down for extra pins for their white capes.

"Isn't this exciting Annie?"

"Your wedding will be exciting Hannah."

Annie didn't bother to explain and Hannah didn't want to ask. She knew how direct her older sister by eleven months could be.

The Forgeher were gathered, ready to seat each guest in their proper place. A few minutes to eight, the male ushers walked to the barn to begin rounding up groups of men for the ceremony. Daniel was one of the first to enter the home. Annie wasn't surprised. She knew Daniel followed the doctrine yet remained open to Annie's interpretation of the ways. Daniel too had a sense about him.

With respective seats being taken and ministers present, Ira's son Jonas announced a hymn number from the Ausbund. Annie, still in the back kitchen, heard his scratchy voice. While she plain just didn't like Ira, she felt even stronger about this son of his. "I've seen him in the city hanging out on street corners with untrusting individuals," she told Daniel more than once. "He's wearing sunglasses and smoking his pipe with girls half dressed and smoking cigarettes."

Annie's heart went out for Mary. Peering into the front room her eyes met her sister's for a brief moment. That shade of navy Mary had chosen hid her large frame which made the contrast between Mary and Ira less noticeable. The white cape seemed to be choking the bride as a look of discomfort overtook her when the ceremony began. With a turn of her head, Mary committed her life to that bit of a man whom Annie considered plain evil. There were no flowers or instruments strum-ming in the background—only hymns and prayers. When the Bishop announced it was time for people to speak up if there were any objections, Annie began whipping potatoes so fast she made herself dizzy. She stopped just in time to witness Bishop Samuel declare Mary and Ira man and wife.

Those potatoes took another beating.

"If you continue you'll be serving mush."

Looking her in the eye, Annie's mother put her hand on her daughter's shoulder. In a whisper so none of the other women cooks could hear, this mother spoke to the core of what this daughter had struggled with ever since being a child and watching the English pass her by, staring at her as if she were some novelty in a sideshow.

"This is your sister's path. Ira will provide for Mary."

"Provide what Mother; more children? Who has decided this is Mary's path? It surely can't be Mary."

"That is the reason of marriage. We accept God's children. His will is not for us to know. It is not for us to question. Today God's will is uniting Ira and Mary as one. They are being shown the way. They have accepted God's will. And you Annie Finley, you keep such thoughts to yourself. I pray that you come to accept your path. Daniel Finley is your husband. Do you forget you stood in that room with Daniel by your side, with that very Bishop proclaiming you man and wife? Accept the fruit of your husband Annie. That is our path as wives. We do not question. We submit to our husbands for they provide the fruit of God's will." And with that said, Annie's mother went into the front room.

That was more than she'd ever said to Annie throughout Annie's twenty-eight years. Communication did not exist between the two.

Others in that summer kitchen had pretended to be stirring or chopping or filling platters but that dialogue between a mother and daughter could not be ignored. They'd strained to catch every word for such words were never spoken, such thoughts never completed. All the women knew Annie was somewhat odd. After all, she and Daniel had produced only one child in eight years of marriage.

Annie stood by the woodstove. Her heart was pounding so hard she barely heard the commotion in the other room with tables being shuffled about and then covered in white cloth.

"Would it be God's will should Mary be in danger?" Annie asked out loud. No one answered. Even if they had the answer they wouldn't speak up. Annie knew that. She wasn't looking for an answer. Actually she didn't even know where the question came from. Pushing back strands of hair that had fallen loose from her bonnet, Annie took stalks of celery and sliced them until they were paper thin. Then with her hands cupped, she picked them up and threw them into a boiling pot.

Annie needed fresh air. Before the serving began, she escaped out behind one of the small buildings. She knew Jacob was being tended to and she was sure Daniel would be enjoying a cigar.

"Someone from the city gave Ira a fancy box of smokes held together by a gold seal," Mary had told Annie the night before. Annie was certain Ira was passing them out. It made for a good show on his part.

Annie was glad to be alone. Growing up, where she stood now was where she used to go to escape her siblings, something most always impossible to do. Snow that had fallen before dawn was mixed in some places with maple and poplar leaves. Some places were pure mud while others blanketed in white. Annie took off her bonnet, undid her hair pins, and let the wind cool her. Sitting on an over-turned bucket, with odd boards piled every which way and chickens squawking at her intrusion, Annie tried to understand her discontent.

"This is Mary's choice, Annie. All you can do is be there for her," said Daniel more than once.

His suggestion that Ira and his thirteen children were part of Annie's discontent was part of it. But Annie knew it was deeper. Watching geese heading south, Annie's confusion took shape. She concluded there was something rotten going on in the community. According to an interview in one of her magazines featuring the woman now running for President, to make a difference you first must get to the root of who you are and what you are trying to achieve. Annie was at the root of her discontent and her instincts told her to beware.

"If that woman wins today I wonder if she'll make the difference she has promised."

That answer would have to wait. Politics were taboo—even on Election Day. Annie would have to keep reading her magazines and newspapers. Intrigue of how things worked outside her limited world was always just below the surface. To think a woman could be the President was empowering to this woman surrounded by chickens while twirling her hair back up around her head.

Deciding she'd best get back, Annie stood, then secured her bonnet in place. Screeching tires drew her attention to the highway far down the gravel road. Three—maybe four—of those sleek, black cars with darkened windshields and shiny polish bolted past her view in an instant. Something most unwelcome was seeping into the community.

The rest of the day flew. One finished meal blended into the next one needing to be prepared. Dishes were washed in tubs. Cakes were served. Gifts observed. Then singing filled that old home. Even Annie joined in with verses from the brown book until noticing Jacob yawning and rubbing his eyes. She knew it was time to leave. She knew Jacob would fall right to sleep in the carriage. Reading would have to wait for another night.

Finding Daniel in the barn, she quietly pulled him aside.

"I will put Jacob's coat on him and we can go Daniel."

It was quite windy now and more snow than rain was falling, covering the road and starting to pile up all over the place.

"Whatever my bride wants," smiled Daniel.

"Then we best get going." Annie pulled Daniel close. "This bride wants her husband."

Goodnights were said as Daniel went for the carriage. Taking Mary aside, Annie held her close. Ira and Mary would stay there this first night as man and wife. But Annie couldn't think of that.

"Be safe Mary."

Buttoning Jacob's coat; then grabbing his blanket, Annie stepped towards the front door.

"Wait Annie." It was Hannah. "You can't forget Bear."

"Thank you. Good night Hannah."

Turning to leave, Annie noted her mother, staring at her as if to say remember my words. Annie said nothing, secure in knowing she didn't have to submit to Daniel. She shared with Daniel; something her mother would never understand.

Along Co. Rt. 68

ANNIE WAS RIGHT. WRAPPED IN HIS favorite blanket and holding Bear, Jacob fell asleep before they reached the end of the dirt road covered in snow. The weather had turned quite nasty. At times the wind became so ferocious that clusters of saturated leaves and twigs and stray pine cones darted towards them through the darkness.

"Pull the tarp up round you Annie, only about two—two and a half miles to go. Is Jacob really asleep?"

Daniel grabbed hold of his black felt hat, deciding to keep it off before losing it to the night. Even with his long coat buttoned to the neck, Daniel was soaking wet. He'd wrapped extra blankets around Annie and Jacob and insisted she sit behind him with Jacob in her lap. That way they'd be better protected from what was going on all around them.

"He had a long day with all those cousins!"

Annie had to yell. Looking into the wind she couldn't tell if it was raining or snowing or from which way it was coming. The side lantern was useless in this weather. Patches of fog crept out onto the highway like oil on water. Annie never liked being on the road at night, especially with Jacob.

"Now he has more cousins!"

"Please don't remind me Daniel."

Rain was coming in torrents now, taking Annie's breath away. Pulling Jacob closer, she peeked to see if he was still warm and dry. Slightly covering his face with his blanket, Annie kissed the tip of his nose while Bear kept him even warmer.

"Look. Look Annie. Must be the Ferguson Farm. Think those are their barns all lit up. Hard to tell but that means we just have the curve ahead; then it's our road."

Annie caught only some of what Daniel was hollering. She didn't have to hear it all. She knew he was reassuring her they'd soon be off the highway and back home. Through splinters of light shed from their neighbors place, Annie eyed flashes of Daniel's silhouette against the foreboding backdrop. How tall and strong he sat, protecting the two that were his life. With his beard drenched and twisted with icy splinters, Daniel held the reins in a firm grasp as he led them through nature's wrath. Annie loved his broad shoulders and the way his wavy, dark brown hair hit the nap of his neck. Annie loved his spirit and his patience. She loved his tenderness and passion. He had a way of making her feel alive.

An even stronger gust of wind brought Annie back to the moment. Fingers of sleet and leaves soaking wet mixed with snow were slamming their way straight through the front of the carriage. Annie could hardly breathe. Her wool cloak was covered in the stuff. Her bonnet was twisted down past her forehead. She tried pulling the tarp back up around her and Jacob but the wind was unrelenting.

"We're almost there Annie." Daniel turned to take a quick look at his family. That would be his last as he led the horse up the knoll before the curve.

It happened as they started down that incline. Daniel made ready for the sharp right then sharp left curve ahead but something scared the horse. She jerked her head straight back over and over again. Annie thought she heard thunder rumbling in the distance. She thought she saw lightning flashing. Annie had no time to question. No time to prepare. For what she'd concluded to be more of nature's elements turned out to be a fast approaching car barreling straight down the middle of the highway. The howling wind howled even louder. The snow now all snow fell even harder. Any sense of direction was lost as Daniel fought to control that horse.

"Hold on to Jacob Annie. Hold him close!"

Daniel was fighting the best he could. With all his strength he tried but it wasn't meant to be. The horse, already spooked, jerked uncontrollably; lunging from one side to another. Daniel began to lose his grip. The horse could feel his weakness as the reins flew wildly into the selfish storm. Rearing back the horse then lunged ahead into the other lane. Headlights on high beam blinded the steed, making her race even more chaotically. Frantic hoofs on the snowy pavement deafened Annie as she desperately cradled Jacob tightly against her.

"Daniel! Daniel!" Annie pleaded through the turmoil. "Daniel!"

There was no answer. There was no Daniel sitting in front, protecting, reassuring. And then, it happened.

Brakes screeched as the horse galloped into that vehicle's path. The smell of Jacob's blanket was the last thing Annie remembered as down went that horse and into the ditch flew the carriage, rolling over and smashing against a thicket of pine and oak.

It kept raining. The snow never quit falling. The north wind continued its yelling. It was as if the night swallowed up the accident and continued to play on. Except for the horn blasting and headlights fixed upon the road, nothing changed nature's course in that split second while fate crossing Annie Finley's path changed her life forever.

Dazed and aching and drenched even more, Annie lay in a field of icy dried-up weeds and snow-covered grass. It seemed like hours but it was only minutes before Annie realized where she was. Playing back those last moments, she tried focusing. She tried grasping the reality of it all. The horn was all she heard pushing through the bleakness. There was no Daniel yelling, no Jacob crying. Where were they? A gut-wrenching anguish overtook her. Annie drew on strength deep within. She had to find her family. She had to hold them and tell them they would be alright.

"Oh my God," she shuttered thinking of her baby somewhere out in the soaking turmoil. "Please keep him safe Lord. Please keep him safe."

Covered in mud and leaves, Annie's face and hands were scratched and bleeding. She tried pulling herself up. She tried standing but her knees buckled, sending her tumbling into more leaves and grime. Throwing her bonnet into the wind and pushing back the sleeves of her cloak, Annie dug into the freezing earth with her fingers, clawing inch by inch back up the slippery embankment. Struggling to concentrate on putting one foot ahead of the other, Annie forced her boots deep into the soil laden with pebbles and cinders sharp as daggers and started creeping back up to the highway. Pellets of ice pounded her face and gnawed at her swollen hands. The groaning wind pushed Annie back but this time nothing could break this determined woman. Struggling to focus on her surroundings once she reached the pavement, Annie laid there collecting her thoughts while regaining her strength. The vehicle had ended up in a field perpendicular to the road. It just missed slamming into some maples. Its headlights cut eerily through the darkness allowing Annie the ability to decipher a most haunting image. It was the horse thrashing against the asphalt. Swirling back and forth nearby was one of the buggy's wheels. That's all Annie could see except for outlines of something close to the wheel. The snow was coming down so heavily that whatever it was, the snow was consuming it. Blaring music from the car's stereo suddenly came at her, making Annie's head pound even more. She tried yelling but nothing came. It'd taken all her might to get back up from the gully.

"I have to get up. I have to."

Flat out on all fours, in the middle of the road, Annie Finley began to pull herself back up on her feet. She had to. She was left with no other choice. It didn't matter that as she inched herself up, the pain shooting out from her left knee nearly crippled her. She bit her lip; dug her fingers against the roadway.

"Why hasn't anyone come by? Why isn't anyone helping me find my baby?"

Teetering on her good knee, Annie took a deep breath, pulling herself up even more while balancing herself against the wind. Once standing, Annie let out curdling cries that remained unanswered. But it didn't matter. Nothing mattered, except for the agony deep within her heart.

Feeling nauseous, taking tiny steps, Annie slid one boot in front of the other. Her hair was wild with knots, both knees were weak and shaking. It probably wasn't more than fifteen to twenty feet back towards whatever it was in the highway but to Annie it might as well have been a mile. She was trembling with worry. Realizing it was up to her, Annie found her voice as she neared the wheel.

"Jacob! Daniel! I'm here. I'm right here. Please tell me where you are. We are going to be okay but please. Please tell me where you are. Please tell me!"

Annie took a breath trying not to think the worse. "Please. I'm here. I love you Jacob. I love you Daniel. My God help me! Someone help us! Please!"

Annie let out a blood curdling scream as she fell back on the old road, landing on her left knee. "Oh no, help me! Where is my baby! Daniel, I need you Daniel. I can't find our baby. Daniel Finley! Help me! Please help me!"

Swirls of snow and dirty leaves flew around her, beside her, on top of her. The brazen, unrelenting wind didn't care about Annie Finley. It seemed to be enjoying her desperation. Hard as she tried, Annie couldn't stop the deluge of tears pouring out once she found herself back on all fours. She could decipher the horse flailing about nearby. Lying with her arms outstretched it was at first hard to figure out what her near frozen fingers were touching. She wiggled them a little more. She did have some feeling. She knew. Instantly she knew it was Daniel's coat. Of course she'd know. She'd made the coat. She'd fitted it to him, pinned each dart and sewed every seam. It was Daniel's coat! It was! Pain didn't matter now. It was Daniel.

Rolling over, Annie crawled to the sopping wet mass that was her husband.

"Oh my God! My dearest Daniel. It's me. It's your Annie. I'm here. Don't worry. I'm here Daniel."

Annie was beyond shaking. Taking deep breaths she tried to

remain calm but the pools of blood on the pavement seeping from Daniel's nose made her nauseous. She couldn't control it. Rolling to the side of the road Annie heaved between screams of despair. Having emptied her stomach, Annie found a strength from which she knew the source. It was God. He was with her. Pulling her cloak off, Annie covered Daniel. Hesitating for an instant she checked for a pulse. Even though her fingers were ice cold and more than numb Annie felt it. She felt it! Daniel was alive! But that momentary glimpse of hope was short lived as the dying horse became uncontrollably erratic, flinging itself closer and closer towards Daniel. That new found strength allowed Annie to react. She knew it'd be best if she didn't move Daniel but she had no choice. Forgetting her knee and her aches and bruises, Annie bent down. Putting her arms through Daniel's, Annie began dragging him away from the horse. She didn't have to go far. The horse collapsed in front of her. Annie could tell Daniel's horse raised since a newborn colt had died.

Still there was no time to waste.

"I must find Jacob Daniel. Stay here my love," Annie whispered. "I love you my Daniel."

But where was the joy of their lives? Could he have slept through this nightmare? Why were there no passersby?

"Think Annie Finley. Think! Concentrate."

Clearing her head, Annie made her way back down to the buggy, thinking maybe Jacob was inside.

"Jacob. It's Mommy Jacob. I'm coming honey. Daddy is sleeping. We love you my little one. If we hurry there's still time to read. We still have time my precious one."

But except for Bear, the carriage was empty."

Gone was reasoning. Gone was the possibility that maybe just maybe her baby was sleeping. This mother needed her child. This mother knew. She knew. Her gut was screeching with loss. Panic seeped into her womb.

"Jacob! Jacob! My God. My dear God give me my son!"

Annie began to hurry. She was going nowhere. She was searching in circles.

"Daniel Daniel. I can't find Jacob. Please help! Please help me!"

Faster she flew. It was as if she'd rid herself of all pain. This mother was in search of her child. Nothing could stop her.

"Jacob. I have Bear. I have Bear, Jacob!"

And then she stopped. In the middle of that frozen bed in wait of winter, Annie saw him. She saw her baby's blonde hair against the white sheet. She knew. God had shown her the way as she had asked him to do. She knew. My God she knew. A mother knows. The joy of her life, her very reason for welcoming each new dawn was in eternal sleep. She just knew.

Falling to her knees, Annie bent down and gently brought him to her. Brushing aside those strands as she always did, Annie cradled her child, kissing the tip of his nose. His sweet angel face was without a scratch. God had taken him back home just as he had given him to Annie and Daniel Finley, perfect in every way. Holding Jacob close and putting one foot in front of the other, Annie made her way back up to Co. Rt. 68. The wind was even more selfish, gnawing at this woman numb with loss. For a moment Annie hesitated, trying to remember where the horse had fallen. That's when a voice sliced the darkness, bellowing with laughter and projecting cusswords one right after another into the night. Then that vehicle's engine was revving and the music turned to a feverish pitch.

"What a ride! What a ride!" It was the driver. He was alive and raring to go, pushing down on the gas pedal, laughing uncontrollably.

Standing in the middle of the road with Jacob in her arms, Annie had no time to think as the car pulled out of the field, heading straight towards her. She stood there. A part of her thought, "Go ahead. Hit me. Put me out of my misery. Send me home to God with Jacob."

But the car crept slowly by as the voice inside ranted about "Those damn Amish—never can see them!"

With a window rolled down the stench of liquor mixed with cigar about toppled Annie. She stood firm, trying to catch a glimpse of the monster at the wheel of one of those sleek black cars with a tinted windshield. It didn't appear to have been damaged but it was impossible to be sure. Even in the dark, Annie could see something shiny hanging from the rear view mirror. She noted a tall shadow of a man with a laugh that echoed no remorse. Suddenly he sped up and headed down the road, disappearing around the curve that would take him past the Ferguson Farm.

The wind had turned, coming from the east now. It'd stopped snowing. Stars were making their debut as Annie cradling Jacob sat on asphalt next to Daniel. Clopping hoofs pulling buggies and distant sirens could be heard approaching. That's the last thing Annie remembered.

The Day After

IT WAS THE AROMA OF STRONG coffee mixed with cornbread that woke Annie. Whisperings and the door opening and closing confused her. Why hadn't Daniel woke her ? It was already light outside. Who was doing the baking she herself should be doing? That's when she decided she'd best get downstairs and tend to her family. Fumbling with blankets, Annie reached over to Daniel's side of the bed. She could tell how long he'd been up by the warmth still left on the sheets. Cold! The sheets were cold! How could that be? Ready to pull at the blankets again, Annie felt something in her way. She knew it was Bear. Panic set in. Bear belonged to Jacob. He always slept with Bear. That's the way the routine went at bedtime.

"Say good night to Daddy Jacob," Annie would say, standing at the bottom of the stairs—one hand holding a book and the other Bear—waiting for Jacob as he gave his father a big hug.

"That's our routine! Bear belongs to Jacob! What is going on?" questioned Annie, pulling herself up, awake enough to realize these were not her blankets and this was not her bed—not even her bedroom. She was back home in her parent's bed! A shooting pain from her left knee crippled Annie as she tried to stand. Flashes of a speeding car and fumes of liquor mixed with cigar smothered her. Wretched in grief, Annie fell to the floor, sobbing. Thrashing from one side to the other, with fists pounding the wood floor, despair overtook this mother—this wife of Daniel Finley. That's when Bear fell next to her and that's when Annie realized she had to go find them. They needed her now more than ever. She was the one that had to be strong for the both of them. Annie found her clothes—now dry and piled on the rocking chair her mother had used for all her many children. Dressing quickly and grabbing Bear, Annie went downstairs.

The house was full of family and strangers. Some were in uniform. Mary was the first to reach her sister.

"Oh Annie. Oh Annie," muttered Mary, shaking so hard that Ira had to take her into the front parlor.

That was fine with Annie. Ira disgusted her as did everyone staring at her.

"Mother; where's my baby? Where's my Daniel? I need to go to them now!" Where did you put my cloak?"

As soon as she asked that question, Annie remembered covering Daniel with it.

"Where is my baby? Where is my Daniel? Please! I have to be with them!"

A rather heavy set man with a wide-brim hat spoke up.

"Mrs. Finley. I'm Sheriff Davis. I realize you must be in shock but I'd like to ask you a few questions so I can wrap up my report."

"Take the sheriff into the kitchen Annie. There's coffee made."

"But I need to know!"

"Jacob is resting at the funeral parlor, Annie," said her mother. "Mr. Ewart said he'd bring Jacob home later today."

"It's God's will young lady," spoke the Bishop. "God has His plan. It's that plan that we accept without question."

As if not hearing the Bishop, Annie turned to her Mother. "Where is Daniel Mother?"

Again the Bishop spoke. "The Fergusons were kind enough to help you. They brought you into their home while Jacob was tended to. They were the ones who called for help. After you speak to the Sheriff, we'll talk about Daniel."

Annie knew what the old Bishop was saying. She knew the Church would decide the extent of Daniel's care. They would be the ones paying for it.

"Where did they take Daniel? Will he be ok? What will my baby be wearing? I am his mother! I decide what he wears to eternal sleep. I am his mother!"

Annie had enough of protocol. It was stifling. My God she'd lost her child. She had no inkling as to Daniel's condition or where he'd been taken.

"I need a horse and if you won't give me a horse I'll walk. I have to find Daniel and tend to Jacob."

"You mustn't be rude Annie. The sheriff and his deputy were kind enough to wait for you." Annie's mother hesitated. "You will be able to clean your child and dress him in traditional white. God willing when Daniel heals our Savior will plant another seed of life within your womb. If ye had submitted —"

"Stop. Stop right there with that sermon Mother."

Turning to the sheriff who was growing increasingly impatient, Annie signaled for him to follow her. The deputy joined them.

"Coffee?" she asked, standing at the woodstove.

"No thanks Mrs. Finley. Your mother was kind enough to give me a cup along with her bread. She is a fine cook for sure."

When Annie didn't respond, the sheriff signaled to the deputy to sit down and take out a notepad.

"I have just a few questions. We've spoken to the Fergusons. We've talked with your family. Care if I have another slice of that bread?"

The sheriff seemed a bit aloof, as if he was going through the motions while wishing he were somewhere else.

"Take the whole loaf," replied Annie, pulling out a chair.

"Okay then. Well I presume the horse must have been spoofed by the weather. What a terrible wind last night. That's what happens when you people travel those roads in the dark. Lanterns don't do the trick. Those passing by aren't given fair warning. Terrible thing you lost the horse—and your child too."

"It was the car that scared our horse. It wasn't the storm. Daniel is a fine horseman no matter what the weather. He'd trained that horse. A

car—one of those black cars that are everywhere—you must know what
I mean—that car caused the accident. The license plate started with TU.
There have to be tire tracks in the field or alongside the road. He sat
there long enough. I could tell he'd been drinking. You must see those
cars on the road. You must!"

The deputy with the notepad wasn't writing down a thing.

"Don't you want to do some investigating? Check for tracks. Don't
you have a database?" Annie asked. "Write this down. A sleek black car.
They're everywhere!"

"I haven't seen any ma'm."

The deputy was not only rude. He seemed more interested in finishing the cornbread than taking notes.

"Ok! It was a black shiny car. That helps us—with something
hanging from the rear view mirror and the first two letters on the license
plate were TU. The man was rather tall and he'd been drinking. Why do
you claim he'd been drinking—Annie?"

"Because Sheriff, I smelled liquor."

"You know the smell of liquor?"

"I also know the smell of pot."

"So was this supposed driver drinking and doing drugs—Annie?"

"That's up to you to find out."

Annie had enough. It was clear these officials dressed in gray were
only doing the basics. This would be labeled an accident. Who cares if
a child died? It was only an Amish child and Amish have lots of other
children.

Not waiting for goodbyes, Annie stood and started through the
doorway.

Pleasantries were exchanged between the Bishop and Sheriff. As he
was about to close the front door, Sheriff Davis turned and spoke to
Annie.

"Let it go Mrs. Finley. Do what you're supposed to do. Take care of
your husband." With that final statement, the door closed.

Before Annie could respond the Bishop took her by the hand and
walked into the kitchen. Standing in the midst of women preparing the

noon meal, the Bishop told Annie that Daniel had been taken to the hospital about eight miles away. He was in a coma with injuries to his spine.

"I have to go to him."

"Your child will need tending to. You must prepare for his burial."

"But Bishop, I have to see Daniel. Jacob is his child too. I have to tell him."

"Daniel can't hear you."

"Yes he can. I believe in God Bishop. I believe God will help me. He will be by my side. He's always by my side, even last night when He called our baby home. I'm going to see my husband even if I have to walk."

Those cutting the vegetables and peeling potatoes heard every word. No one ever told the Bishop what they were doing against his will.

"I'll wait to hear how you find Daniel. Then we will decide what we will do for him."

"I'll be home later tonight. Mother—I need a buggy—now."

"Let me help you get ready Annie. Can I help Annie Mother?" Hannah asked.

"Yes Hannah. Help your sister. I think it best if you stay at Annie's while she goes to the hospital. I'll bring food. Others may stop by. Pray Annie. Do as the sheriff suggested. Accept the will of God."

"I accept His will. It's actions of others that I do not accept."

"We are not to question. We are to forgive Annie."

"I forgive those who are forgiving Mother."

Tired of trying to talk to her daughter who always had to have the last word, Annie's mother handed her a cloak Mary had made for their grandmother. The old woman passed away before she could wear it.

Moments later the sisters were on their way with Bear sitting between them. Some of the snow had melted, leaving puddles alongside the road. Neither spoke a word. Passing by the Ferguson Farm and going down and around those fateful curves, Annie pulled back on the reins.

"It looks so different. It's as if it never happened. There's the field where my baby died. And it's as if it never happened."

"Remember what Mother said Annie. Please Annie."

Pulling farther back on the reins, the buggy came to a halt where Annie calculated the point of impact.

"Look at the tire marks on the road. Even with the snow last night, there were tire marks. There are still tire tracks in the field."

Jumping down from her seat, Annie started towards the middle of the highway.

"Annie. Please. This won't help anyone."

"It could if the sheriff bothered to do his job."

Trying to remember where that car came to a rest, Annie started to scuff the area with her right foot. Bending down, Annie pulled something out from a clump of matted weeds. Shoving it into her pocket, she decided to look at it later. The sound of screeching tires from an approaching vehicle alerted her to take action.

"Get farther off the road Hannah. Hurry, Hannah!"

As Annie jumped into the buggy now moving further down into the field, one of those sleek, black cars with tinted windows went racing by.

Annie watched as it became but a speck on the horizon.

"What did you find Annie?"

"I thought it was something but it was nothing."

Without another word Annie took the reins, making it home before noon.

Jumping out of the buggy, Hannah told Annie to take her time. She'd take care of things until Annie returned.

Everywhere Annie looked there were reminders of how her life had forever changed. Someone besides Daniel had tended to the horses. Someone had chopped the wood. Annie felt like screaming. Daniel was the one who tended to the horses. Daniel was the one who chopped the wood. Passing by the school sitting back from the road, Annie could no longer hold back her grief. Some of the children were outside playing. Some were Jacob's cousins. They stopped when they saw Annie. They stood in silence. Annie kept going, letting the tears spill out like water overflowing a levee. Something triggered her memory. Annie remembered the object she'd shoved in her pocket.

"I'm sorry for lying God." Annie knew if she told Hannah she'd found something, Hannah would tell their Mother. She told her everything. She was afraid not to.

Annie studied the object now in her hand. It was a cufflink; a sterling silver cufflink with the initials TU engraved on the front.

"I'll find you TU. On the grave of my son I vow I will find you."

A sign told Annie she had less than six miles to go. She'd be home in time to tend to Daniel's other duties.

The Aftermath

IF ANNIE SCRUBBED THE KITCHEN WALLS one more time it was possible they might cave in. Anything was possible after living the nightmare of the last few weeks. Tests showed Daniel suffered an acute blow to his spinal column. Hooked up to more tubes and machines than Annie could count, he remained in a coma. Doctors were hesitant predicting his outcome. The decision would soon be made as to whether or not to move him to a health center specializing in trauma injuries. The Bishop told Annie the day after Jacob's burial that the Church would help Daniel all they could.

"He's a firm member of the flock. He provides for his family. He contributes to his community."

The elder's words haunted Annie. Not that she doubted God's will. She doubted her ability to get from one day to the next. Going against the rule of the community, Annie visited Jacob before the world woke up most every morning. He was buried near an apple tree in the last row of the cemetery situated at the end of a dirt road the locals called Horseshoe Lane. She'd only missed one day and that's after the horses broke through the fence in the back pasture. She found all of them. Two had sustained such severe injuries that Annie had to put them down. One was Jacob's horse.

Annie never did get out of bed the next day. Over and over she relived the funeral. Faces of all who visited kept surfacing in her mind. Hannah had asked to stay with her the two nights before Jacob was put to rest but Annie refused her company. Instead, Annie slept on the floor in front of the pine box holding her baby. She wanted to be alone with her child. She read to him until the wee hours.

Of course there were no flowers; no eulogy. Annie put Jacob's favorite book with him, along with that blanket she'd made when he was a newborn. No one knew. This too was against protocol as was the anger and need to avenge her child's death.

When in town one day, Annie stopped to ask Sheriff Davis if there was anything happening with the investigation. She knew the answer before asking. She knew there was no investigation. Annie wanted to stop at the library to ask for help using a computer. She'd read about something called Google where all you had to do was type in what you wanted to know and it would tell you. But there was no place to tie the horse and a part of her was not ready to learn about "TU". That time would come sooner than she realized.

A Knock on the Door

THANKSGIVING WEEK CAME DESPITE ANNIE'S DENIAL it existed. How could she give thanks when she felt empty? She told Elizabeth not to count on her for the traditional feast the next day. She'd told her the same thing the day Hanna was married. She stayed home with the door locked.

This year Annie's Thanksgiving would be visiting Daniel. On the way home, she'd be with Jacob when everyone else was gathered in celebration. Annie never told Daniel about the two horses she had to shoot. Instead she described the sunsets spreading across the back fields. She talked about the birds frequenting the feeder Jacob had made last spring and how the creek remained free of ice even though the temperature had dropped below freezing several times. Over and over she told him not to worry.

At first Annie thought what she was hearing downstairs was a limb of the old oak tree scratching at the window. After all, who'd be visiting with so much to do for tomorrow's holiday? Two of her brothers had already stopped to see if Annie needed any help. They didn't stay long. Annie was quite apt in the barn.

Sitting on the edge of Jacob's bed, she rationalized that if she stayed still, if in fact someone was at the door, they'd go away. But what turned out to be knocking at the door only got louder. Peeking from atop the stairs she noted two shadows looming on the front porch. Her heart quickened, thinking it might be the sheriff. Putting Bear back in place on Jacob's pillow Annie descended the stairway.

Even before she opened the door, Annie could smell the perfume. It belonged to the women from the city. For a brief second Annie wanted to run—somewhere—anywhere. She didn't have the strength to discuss colors and patterns. She didn't give a damn about her quilts.

"Annie! I see you Annie. Let us in. We're freezing!"

It was the taller of the two, ready to open the door herself. Annie beat her to it.

"Gosh girl it's cold out there. How do you stand it?"

"Annie Finley! So happy you're home. Were you sleeping?"

Both women rushed inside, heading directly to the woodstove.

"Oops. These are for you Annie. I don't want to burn the place down!"

Setting a cardboard box on the table the one called Alicen turned back around to warm up.

"It's full of magazines Annie. We know you like to keep up with the news so we brought all we could find with our new President on the cover. Did you hear? She won! We have a woman President—Hispanic at that! She did it Annie!" There was a pause in the one-way conversation. "Annie? What's wrong? Where's Jacob? We brought him his favorite cookies—the double fudge ones."

Annie didn't move. She couldn't speak. Logs crackling broke the silence.

The women sensed the sadness. It was in every corner of that home.

"Let's sit down." Both women led Annie to the oak table. As the early afternoon sun tiptoed about the kitchen, the nightmare of the last few weeks was put into words and as Annie spoke the stronger she became.

"I'll make us some hot chocolate," she said as both women sat wiping their eyes.

"How do you do it Annie? I would crumble if anything happened to my child."

"I have to be the strong one Alicen."

Pouring the boiling water into cups, Annie continued. "I've been told I must accept God's will. But if I am to accept the will of God I must first understand it. I try to put it all together but I don't have all the pieces Heather."

"What do you mean?" asked the curly-haired redhead.

"There was no investigation. It was determined an accident without question. The Sheriff knew there'd be no questions. We Amish don't question. We accept in silence. Then we go back and have more children."

Annie explained about the black car causing the accident and how it was the same type of car frequenting not only Ira's farm but others too. She told of seeing young men from communities in other states lingering about and then disappearing.

"And there's the cufflink matching the license plate."

"Cufflink?" questioned Heather.

"Yes. I found it in the field the day after the accident."

"And the license plate?"

"I was afraid he would run us over. He slowed down—staring as many do when passing us by. He smelled of liquor and cigars. It was so dark. I tried getting the license number but could only see the first two letters. But I know they matched the cufflink. And there was something shiny dangling from his rear view mirror."

"My gut tells me it's all connected. Can we see the cufflink?" Alicen loved mysteries.

Pulling a piece of cloth out of her pocket, Annie explained, "I don't want to lose this."

Once unwrapped, Annie placed the object in front of her visitors.

"It is worth a pretty penny. That's one expensive diamond between those custom designed letters. It looks like a logo. It reminds me of something. Does it you Heather?"

Getting a closer look, Heather nodded. "I'll be right back."

Before Annie could slice a loaf of pumpkin bread, Heather was back at the table with her laptop.

Pointing to Heather's fancy phone, Annie remarked "I've seen those in the magazines. Can you get to Google with them?"

"Google?"

"Yes. I've read Google can tell you anything you want to know."

"You're exactly right, Annie. And yes, this will take me to Google."

Heather was the technical half of the business, responsible for their website. She was also the numbers person. Alicen had the eye for choosing what would sell and the creativity to market it. Annie's quilts were top sellers. Between the quilts and Daniel's custom-made furniture, the young Amish couple had put away a considerable amount of money, not in the bank but up in the hayloft. Although they contributed their share to the community, they never acknowledged what they kept for themselves. Now she was thankful for that.

Headquartered in the City, the two women were on their way to meet a wooden toymaker near Bangor. With Christmas just 4 weeks away they were pushing it. If it hadn't been for a competent staff they never would have left. They'd planned on stopping at Annie's just long enough to give her the magazines. They were unaware of Annie's loss.

"What are you looking for?" continued Annie.

"I want to know what the design on that cufflink means. I too have seen it before. It's more like a logo."

"Logo?"

"It's a specific design created for a certain business—team—or even school. Logos go on anything, even cufflinks."

Annie was intrigued by this machine that knew everything. It didn't take long. There it was. Right there inside a home void of electricity yet hooked up to the world.

"What did you find Heather?" Annie moved closer as did Alicen

"It's on the Times Union invoices I pay."

"Times Union?"

"It's a group of newspapers Annie. I place ads in them and Heather writes the checks."

"There's more than one paper?" Annie needed to know.

"They have several publications. Some are dailies. Some come out weekly. They're centered in the bigger cities. Circulation for some used to be in the millions."

"So the cufflink could have come from someone at any of them?"

"No. Each publication has their specific logo. You just have to know the clue."

Before Annie could get the question out, Alicen explained. "Each design is the same—except for the stone. This is a dynasty—a newspaper conglomerate. The Morris family has been in the business for generations. They're cutthroat when it comes to breaking a story. They hate to be beaten. They remain news driven despite dwindling ad revenues due to both the internet and the economy. To this day, they're known as "The Jewel in Newspaper Publishing." Each paper has its own specific jewel in its logo. This cufflink—with its ruby center—means it's the Philadelphia Times Union. I should know. I've given them enough business."

"Why are so many of their cars passing through here?" wondered Annie

"That remains a mystery," Heather replied. "Maybe the Times Union is a story all its own."

"I think the only way to find out is to go there," said Annie.

"Where?"

"Philadelphia."

"You want to go to Philadelphia?"

"Yes Alicen—after I tend to Daniel."

"I don't mean to belittle you Annie for you have more strength than I could ever have—but they'd eat you up and throw you out."

"So what if she were to go in disguise?" suggested Heather.

"I don't understand."

"We'll take her to the City and give her a makeover Alicen."

"But what would she do in Philly? How could she exist? She needs more than good looks."

"Tommy will help us. Annie could stay with him."

"What would she do? How could she get around? She'll need a job!"

"I will work at that newspaper."

"You what? How?"

"Teach me about Google."

"You want to learn how to use the computer?"

"Yes—as soon as possible Alicen. Then I will go to that newspaper and be a writer."

"Just like that with no experience. No resume. Walk through the door and you're hired."

"I am a writer. I've been writing since I was a young child. I'd hide my notebooks from my mother in the grain shed. But with Daniel, I would read to him after Jacob went to bed. Daniel would sit by the lamp in the front room. I'd sit beside him on the floor and read, sometimes late into the night."

"What did you write?"

"Stories, some were fiction and some were about those in our community. I even wrote stories for little ones."

"Annie, there are so many who call themselves writers. The odds of that paper hiring you without experience are nil. Seasoned writers find it hard. Competition is fierce even with a degree. And being a reporter involves more than writing."

"I will be hired. If I have to, I will use my female factor. I do understand how such things work. I will think of Jacob and Daniel and why I am there and use what God has given me."

"I believe you will Annie," said Alicen. "We need a plan."

"Daniel has to be part of the plan."

"You said they are considering transferring him?"

"They gave me information to read. They included different locations around. . . ."

She stopped and ran upstairs, returning with a manila envelope. Annie hesitated, sifting through several slick flyers,

"Yes, here it is. I will take Daniel to Temple Health Center. He'll be with me in Philadelphia."

"Of course! That facility is renowned for spinal injuries and get this—they carry some of our best-selling items in their gift shop. I meet with the manager at least six times a year."

"The Bishop said money would be no problem."

"That's one good thing. I can't imagine the price tag without insurance," remarked Heather.

"That is the Bishop's responsibility. The doctors tell me Daniel's recovery is promising."

"No one will question your going to Philadelphia?"

"I've made my intentions clear to the Bishop, Heather. I will be going to help care for my husband. The crops are in; the cellar stocked. One good thing about having so many brothers and sisters is that they can tend to the horses. There's more than enough hay. No one needs to be told about the newspaper. They haven't lost a child."

Filling the plate with more bread and the cups with hot chocolate, Annie asked about Tommy.

"He grew up next door to us outside of Chicago. He and my brother Eddie were best friends. They lost touch after graduation. Tommy had a flair for art and that's what he pursued. Eddie went into the military. He made a career of it."

Heather paused, taking a drink. "Sadly his career cost him his life. Eddie was killed in a mortar attack near Baghdad. Tommy showed up for his funeral. We kept in touch. In my travels I'd become friends with a gallery owner in Philadelphia. I flew Tommy there to meet with him and he's been in that Old City District ever since. He's made quite a name for himself, hosting exhibits and being written up in all the right places. I know he'd help you Annie anyway he could."

"'Our plan is taking shape," Alicen added. "I wish we had more time to spend with you Annie. We could teach you about the internet. You'll need to be knowledgeable in all aspects of the computer just to get through the front door."

"I will go to the library near Daniel's hospital. I've spent time there when I've needed to take a moment. There's a sign at the front desk telling about computer classes three afternoons a week. I will explain my need to keep track of my quilt business. That's all they need to know. Sometimes we get lost in detail. Belief is the key. The rest will fall into place. God is by my side. He understands what I need to do."

"You simplify life so eloquently."

"There is much I question Heather. Yet there remains much that I've been born into that I accept. Simplicity is one."

"Too bad we couldn't have the best of both worlds," remarked Alicen.

"I believe we can," Annie spoke, picking up the cups and putting them in the sink.

"I think we should give Annie a cell phone. We keep one as an extra but we never use it. We need to keep in touch. I assume you know about cell phones too?" Heather asked.

"Yes. I can plug it in when I am at the hospital."

After giving Annie a quick course on the cell, Heather nailed the details.

"Once Daniel is moved, I'll fill Tommy in and let him know when to expect you. He'll do the rest. He has connections. Your travel arrangements will be made through our business. We'll meet you in the City as soon as Daniel is settled. Then we will take you back to Philadelphia a new woman. You stay on the computer. And please Annie—keep in mind you may never fit all those pieces together."

"I will spend much time in the library," Annie replied. "I know what you are telling me but I must fit those pieces together for Jacob and Daniel."

"You are a strong, talented woman Annie Finley. Do this for yourself too."

A knock at the door with a gruff voice calling for Annie interrupted Heather.

"Welcome, Bishop," spoke Annie recognizing the visitor before she opened the door. Towering in the doorway, the squinty-eyed man surveyed what was going on in this humble setting.

Annie knew what he was doing. "Please come in Bishop."

His presence changed the tone of conversation in that kitchen with window panes laced in frost.

"My intention is not to interrupt." Eyeing the fancy phone and notepads, he approached the table.

"You're not interrupting. We were just finishing," Annie explained, introducing the women who returned pleasantries while packing up.

"Mrs. Finley is one of our most talented quilters. Her items are best sellers," spoke Alicen grabbing her coat.

As if not hearing the comment, the Bishop wished the women a safe journey.

"Don't forget this. We have no need for such a thing." Handing that cell phone intended for Annie to Alicen, the elder walked over to the woodstove, rubbing his gloves together.

"Thank you," spoke Alicen as Heather signaled to Annie they'd leave the phone in the barn.

"Good-bye Mrs. Finley. We'll stop back in the spring."

"The Lord willing" was Annie's reply, shutting the door.

The Bishop only stayed minutes. His intent was clear. He'd stopped to urge Annie to attend tomorrow's Thanksgiving with her family.

The next day she made it seem it was because of his urging that she changed her mind. But it wasn't. It was the plan shared between three women that brought Annie to her mother's table. That was her reason for giving thanks.

Thanksgiving

THE STRINGING OF BLINKING LIGHTS AROUND homes always seemed a strange English custom to Annie. But this year she had more on her mind. Annie didn't even notice the lights as the buggy carried her home.

The day had gone better than she'd imagined it would. She'd made Jacob's favorite noodles just as she always did. She brought Bear with her. Believing God's will had spoken, none of the adults discussed the accident. Some of the younger ones did. They missed Jacob. When it was time to eat, Annie sat with Jacob's cousins.

There was no feast for Daniel today thought Annie as she approached the Ferguson Farm on her way back home. When she'd visited him earlier in the morning, his nurse told her Daniel had been restless during the night. He was given a shot to calm him down. He was mumbling something but no one could figure out what he was trying to say.

Annie felt so helpless. She signaled for the horse to hurry. She wanted to get past this part of the road. She wished there was another way home. A few minutes later she was turning onto the gravel path covered in snow that led to the farmhouse. The sun was setting through clusters of cornstalks as Annie unhitched the buggy and led the horse to its stall, bedding him down as Daniel always did. For some reason the thought of Ira came to mind. She'd tried to ignore him. Once she almost asked where his oldest son was on this day of family gathering. Mary told her the young man was away quite often but Mary never asked where he went. Visualizing Mary sharing the same bed with Ira revolted Annie. He attempted discussing the accident after dinner but Annie walked away. Annie felt he was somehow involved. She thought he probably was aware of who the driver of that sleek black car was. Never mind Ira, Annie thought as she headed out of the barn. His day will come. A strange sound interrupted her disdain. It was a ringing—a shrill sound cutting through the cold.

"That phone; my cell phone is ringing!"

Annie ran back into the barn. She'd forgotten Heather hid the phone. By the time she reached it up in the hayloft the ringing stopped but not for long.

"Hello! Hello!"

"You don't have to shout Annie!"

"Heather?"

"Yes Annie. You sound out of breath."

After explaining she'd been racing around looking for the phone, Annie told Heather that based on conversations with Daniel's doctors, the Bishop had given permission for him to be transferred.

"Now we can make those arrangements. I'll tell Daniel's doctor I'd prefer Philadelphia."

"What if they don't agree?"

"They will Heather."

"I'm certain they will!"

With that Annie said good-night. She was tired. Her heart ached for the two missing from her side. Sitting alone up in that hayloft, holding on to Bear, Annie looked out past the pine grove and beyond the rolling fields.

"Good night, my dear angels. Good night. Keep them safe Lord. Please understand what I am about to do is for the two of them. They will always be in my heart wherever this journey takes me."

Snow fell as Annie climbed down the ladder, and headed toward the house. Once inside, she added wood to the fire and soon went to bed. She lay there, remembering how Jacob loved it when it snowed big snowflakes like tonight. They'd bundle up and go out and gather snow in a pitcher. Back inside Annie would add powdered milk. They'd sit and drink the sugar and sweet cream until there was nothing left. Annie never fell asleep until after 3.

Getting Ready

TIME WAS SCREAMING BY. COMPUTER LESSONS were going well. A young man probably not more than 14 was the instructor. The reason they met later in the afternoon was because he was still in school. There were only two others in the class. Neither questioned the presence of an Amish woman. They found it intriguing.

Annie took to the computer as if she had a tech degree. Her writing became crisper. She enjoyed being able to change, delete and start over with a push of a button.

Between lessons and chores, she'd meet with a team of doctors. When the Bishop was absent, Annie lobbied the group for Philadelphia. She reasoned the support she and Daniel would receive from family nearby would be most helpful. This was really a stretch. Family lineage stemmed from Indiana.

Three days before Christmas Annie was told Daniel would be flown by helicopter to Temple the beginning of the following week. All the arrangements, including Annie's travel with Daniel were in place. While the timing was on target, Annie explained the use of a helicopter was against Amish teachings. The Bishop would never approve. A few hours later, plans were set. Daniel would be transferred by ambulance.

With the date pinpointed Annie began to ready herself. She entrusted Hannah with checking the house and her brothers with caring for the horses and keeping watch over the farm. Despite her feelings towards Ira, Annie stopped to say good-bye to Mary the day before her departure. She wasn't surprised to see two of those black cars parked near the outhouses. Heading up the front steps, Annie caught Ira peering out from the barn. He watched until Mary opened the door. Annie didn't stay long—but long enough to again tell her sister to stay safe. Her last stop that afternoon was the cemetery. Annie didn't care who saw her. She knew God understood. After all, he'd given her Jacob in the first place. Sitting by his gravesite with Bear, Annie told him of the snow piling up behind the house. She made sure he knew how many birds were at his feeder. She repeated over and over how much he was loved. When she arrived back home her mother was waiting.

"We missed you on Christmas, Annie."

"I spent the day with Daniel, Mother."

"You must spend all your time with your husband. I haven't seen you since Thanksgiving."

"That is my duty. Isn't it Mother? My duty is to serve thy husband."

Ignoring that remark, Annie's Mother continued, "If you leave tomorrow you will miss Epiphany."

"I didn't make the arrangements Mother. I'm sure the others will gather with you to celebrate the Wise Men's journey."

"I will pray for you on your journey."

That was all they shared that cold December day.

Quite nervous, with much on her mind, Annie made herself a cup of tea with toast. She began packing a bag. She decided to leave Bear on Jacob's bed. She didn't know what she might encounter. She didn't know if she'd be back.

With the wood box full and the house in order, Annie tidied up the kitchen and filled the feeder. She had to be at the hospital before dawn. Her brother John would be taking her. About to go up to bed, she heard that gruff voice again at her door.

"Bishop. Please, come in." Annie held the door as the preacher made his entrance.

"Would you like a cup of tea? The water is still hot."

"I thank you for your offer but I must get back. I stopped to give you this." Handing Annie an envelope, the Bishop continued. "It gives you the information necessary for Daniel's hospitalization and an allotment to get by. I will keep in touch."

Putting his gloves back on, something caught his eye. It was Annie's cell phone lying on the table.

"I found it in the snow. John is going to mail it after he takes me to the hospital." That was the best Annie could come up with as the Bishop picked up the cell and stood inches away from her.

"And be ye not conformed to this world but be ye transformed by the renewing of your mind that ye may prove what is good and acceptable—and perfect the will of God."

Lifting Annie's right hand to his, the Bishop put the phone in her palm—and left.

Waiting to hear the horse and buggy going back down the pathway, Annie packed the cell in her bag, along with the money she and Daniel had hidden in the barn. She'd give it to Heather for safekeeping. Taking hold of the lamp, Annie went upstairs. After securing the windows and tucking Bear in, she closed Jacob's bedroom door and went to bed.

"Forgive me for trickery Lord. Guide me through what lies ahead." Annie's prayer for understanding drifted through the night as snow cream snowflakes gently fell.

The Journey Begins

"PLOWS HAVEN'T BEEN OUT YET ANNIE. Anything I can carry?"

Without saying a word Annie handed John a bag. He went back outside. Standing in the kitchen, Annie, wrapped up in her grandmother's cloak, took one more look around; then walked out the door.

Despite the drifting snow, they made good time. Not many words were spoken between the brother and sister who'd never had a real conversation anyway. Dawn was breaking as John nudged the horse up the circular drive.

Jumping down off the buggy, Annie turned to grab her bag.

"Plenty of potatoes in the cellar John. Squash too."

"Annie." John paused. "Annie I've seen you at the cemetery. I'll stop some evenings and sit with Jacob."

Where had this older brother been when they were growing up she wondered, standing there as snow fell all around her?

"If you feel comfortable in doing so John. God be with you."

That's all she could get out as she walked through a revolving door and up six flights of stairs.

"Morning Mrs. Finley. We're about ready."

Annie went to Daniel's side. She had so much to tell him. With nurses all about preparing him for the trip, Annie decided to wait. They had a long ride ahead of them.

Moments later a team of doctors huddled about Daniel.

"Your husband will be in good hands. I wish you and Daniel the very best."

Signing a clipboard of papers, the doctor who appeared to be in charge finalized Daniel's departure.

As soon as the doctors left, in came men dressed in identical clothing.

"Mr. Finley is ready," spoke a nurse. "This is the patient's wife—Annie Finley. She will be accompanying her husband to Philadelphia."

To Annie's surprise it didn't take long to transfer Daniel to the ambulance. Once secured, the vehicle, complete with a medical team and Annie in a back seat, departed.

"Snow's letting up," announced the driver. "We'll make Philly in no time."

It turned out the driver's prediction was correct. Once on 81 the highway was bare.

"It's a straight drive now," he stated. "I've made this trip before; mostly farm accidents though."

Annie had never been past the county line. Now the world was whizzing by at top speed; farmland turning into hamlets; then cities and farmland again as valleys led through mountains. They stopped only once—to refuel and stretch their legs. Signs along the highway kept telling Annie they were almost there. After awhile she didn't need them. It was obvious something was ahead as traffic increased and buildings turned into towering giants. It was just as her magazines depicted. Cars and trucks zigzagged above them; all around them. Horns tooted. Lights flashed. Women with spike-heeled boots and hair streaked different colors hurried along in the cold.

Noting the medical team was tending to Daniel with increased attention Annie knew the health center was approaching.

"We're on N. Broad," spouted the driver, veering toward the exit ramp; then following signs to the Health Sciences Center.

Once the ambulance came to a stop, a flurry of professionals appeared. Staying out of the way, Annie waited until they were wheeling Daniel into the building. Annie followed in silence.

In less than an hour those who'd brought Daniel to Philadelphia were back on the road. Annie had been told tests would begin in the morning.

"Mrs. Finley?"

"Yes?"

"I have a message for you." A middle-aged woman with short cropped hair handed Annie a folded piece of paper. "If you need a phone, my desk is right down the hall."

Content Daniel was resting comfortably, Annie stepped outside the room. The message was short. "Go see Pauline at the gift shop. Heather."

"Gift shop?" Annie questioned out loud.

"Need help Mrs. Finley?" It was the woman at the desk.

"I have to go to the gift shop?"

"No problem. Walk to the end of this hall—take a right—then a quick left. You'll see the elevators. Take one going down to the main floor. The gift shop is up passed the coffee shop on the left."

Confusion must have been written all over Annie's face.

"I'll take you down. Sounds easy—but I've worked here over 20 years."

Annie followed the woman.

"Would you like me to wait?"

"I'll be fine," replied Annie, moving out of the way as others entered the shop. "Thank you for your help."

It's like learning the back roads thought Annie, walking through the doorway. Once you've been down them, you remember your way back.

Racks of magazines drew Annie's attention as she stepped up to the counter and asked for Pauline.

"She's out back. I'll go find her." The young man with a bow tie and pleasant smile sprinted through a swinging door, returning in seconds.

"Pauline said she's been waiting for you," he informed Annie, holding the door.

Realizing it must have been her dress that gave her away, Annie stepped into the backroom.

"Over here. I'm up on the ladder.

Inching her way around stacks of boxes, Annie found a graying, slightly overweight woman with hair falling past her waist and big hoop earrings.

"I try keeping this place straight. I love to organize Annie—and I love to talk—my husband tells everyone." And talk she did all the while climbing down the ladder.

Greeting Annie with a warm hug, Pauline led Annie to a small table. They sat down.

"Heather told me about your terrible loss Annie; of your husband's injuries and your plan to get to the bottom of those you feel responsible. I've come up with a way to help you. See that little room. That will be yours. I'll alert everyone here that is *your* space. When you visit your husband you will be coming dressed a little differently than you are now once you land a job! Everything you will need is in there. Come take a look."

Pauline was right. Anything Annie would need to make the change from working woman to simplicity was in front of her; exact replicas of what she was wearing right down to her boots.

"How did you do this?"

"Alicen used her connections."

After exchanging cell numbers, Pauline informed Annie that Heather had booked her on a flight to New York the following evening.

"They'll take you shopping and have you back the next day. You'll be staying with me tonight and tomorrow afternoon I'll take you to the airport."

Annie thought how flying was against Amish beliefs. But that was only for a second, remembering why she had to do this her way. She said a little prayer for forgiveness—and understanding.

New York City

ANNIE THOUGHT FOR SURE ONCE ABOVE the clouds the stars would seem closer. But they didn't. In fact the flight was so short she barely had time to take in the view. The man sitting beside her pointed out the Statue of Liberty; then proceeded to recite its history. She knew it had been a gift but she never let on. Approaching JFK, it seemed to Annie as if the earth and sky were one. She'd left Daniel feeling reassured after doctors told her there would be surgery. A time had not yet been determined as it depended on Daniel. His chances for a full—but slow—recovery were good. Follow-up at the hospital with physical therapy would be necessary. Knowing this made her mission in New York easier. She knew what she had to do, and as the plane landed, she was anxious to get started.

"It's been a pleasure talking with you Mrs. Finley. I must say I was surprised to find an Amish woman sitting next to me."

Annie knew what the gentleman was getting at. She acted as if she didn't. The flight hadn't been long enough to go into details.

"It was a pleasure talking with you Mr. Farrell." Annie stood, waiting to retrieve her bag. That was the last she saw of the man.

Acting as a seasoned traveler, Annie navigated her way amongst the throngs. Alicen had given her explicit directions but she never told her about the moving walkway; zooming people along at an accelerated speed. Why don't they walk faster if they're in that much of a hurry Annie wondered?

Reaching the ground floor, Annie found a seat near the information desk. Whichever door Heather came in, Annie would see her. The glut of buses and taxicabs alongside the curb intrigued Annie; as did the conveyor belts full of luggage. Most amazing—no one stared at her. She blended in with this hodgepodge of humanity.

Absorbed in people watching, Annie wasn't aware of Heather sitting beside her.

"I see you're taking it all in!"

"Heather! How could I have missed you?"

"I'm still in awe of this city. Can't imagine how you must feel."

"I can't put it into words."

"You haven't seen anything yet."

"I read Times Square is the crossroads of the world."

"That's true."

"I understand people skate at Rockefeller Center."

"They do!"

With sirens interrupting their conversation and a light evening snow falling, flashes of that night on Co. Rt. 68 clouded Annie's thoughts. This happened on occasion. Sometimes the images were so vivid—the horse flailing in pain; her baby limp in her arms.

"Do you have a bag Annie?"

"Right here," she replied as thoughts of Jacob playing rabbit with his cousins drifted back to memory.

"Is that the only one?"

"Yes. I travel light!"

"You won't be returning to Philadelphia light."

Sharing a laugh, the two women stood, proceeding out the door and into mass mania.

"How do you know where to go?"

Maneuvering the traffic, Heather explained, "You drive like you're one of them or they'll eat you up."

Vehicles swarmed the highway, swerving in and out; rushing over bridges and through winding tunnels. Then suddenly there it was. Annie knew where she was now. *That* skyline lit the darkness.

"Welcome to New York City, Annie Finley."

The Makeover

CHORES WERE NOT THE REASON THIS time for Annie to be up early. Taking in a view defining the term skyscrapers was the motivation. In the distance the Hudson could be seen glistening in the morning light. Below, the rush continued. Exhaust from vehicles and horns tooting mingled with people in a hurry. So many people—some in fur coats; others alone, shivering in the cold. A policeman on horseback seemed out of place to Annie. But then, so did she.

Heather had given Annie the bedroom of her small apartment located on the top floor of a turn-of-the-century brownstone. Compact described it, with the kitchen blending into an eating area. Heather not only sold Amish ware; she filled her apartment with it.

Annie eyed vendors entering little shops and men in suits and women in heels rushing along. Most were holding coffee cups. Some were walking dogs.

"I can't believe I slept in." Heather was awake, sitting up on the pull-out, rubbing her eyes. Curly red hair was everywhere. "I apologize. I'm not the best hostess."

"You have been quite generous Heather—giving me your bed; making me feel at home."

"I'm glad you're comfortable Annie. Did you get some breakfast?"

"No. I've been too busy looking out the window. It's true when they say New York never sleeps."

"My mother often reminds me that I was the child who could never get enough sleep. Ironic that I live here isn't it?"

"From what I've seen I understand why you do."

Time was ticking. Beds were made; bagels eaten. The plan was to meet Alicen 10:30 sharp at their Mid-Town office. Although partners, their tastes were opposites. Heather preferred Chelsea. Alicen called the Upper Eastside home.

"We'll get coffee on the way. Sure you don't want to wear something of mine?"

"When it is time I change I will do so. But thank you for the offer."

Except for those running by in skintight attire plugged into iPods, Annie kept up with the morning rush. She found it exhilarating. A few times she had to stop and wait for Heather.

Noting street signs she'd only read about, Annie got into the rhythm of the City until she heard Heather shouting her name.

"Annie! You have to experience a Starbucks."

"Last I read they're downsizing."

"It's that timing thing again."

"I never understood why they have to be located on so many corners," spoke Annie as Heather led the way. "If they are as good as I've read, people would seek them out."

"You have a mind for business Annie."

"I look through humble eyes which I'm beginning to appreciate."

Fascinating to Annie were those sitting at small tables sipping their brew—absorbed in their computers while others read the Times.

Heather tried talking Annie into a Frappuccino but she preferred a coffee—black with a touch of sugar. With no time to waste, they took their coffees to go. Hailing a cab, they were on their way to meet Alicen. They found her on the phone with a client.

Heather took the opportunity to show Annie around the operation located inside what used to be an abandoned mercantile building. It drew the curious; making the list of "Fascinating Little Places to Visit in the

Big Apple". Twice a week tours were given of the property—ending in a charming gift shop. Annie saw her quilts displayed about old hutches unfinished. Everyone remarked on their quality. After landing the client and signing some papers, Alicen was ready to join in Annie's transformation.

Heather had the connections. She'd alerted the owner of a chique Soho boutique to be ready—from casual clothing to designer labels, plus accessories, shoes to boots. Every mood; every situation including sheer lingerie and sensual perfumes had to be considered. If Annie was going undercover, she'd have to be prepared for the unexpected.

After introductions were made, clothes were brought into Annie. Once a size was determined it all came together. And when she stepped out from behind the curtain the store became silent.

"Did I put something on incorrectly?" Thinking it was the jeans or boots or the brown leather jacket over the crisp white blouse, Annie explained "This is how they do it in the magazines. That's why I added the pearls. Too much?"

Reaching up, Annie pulled out her hairpins, releasing her long, rich ebony hair.

"You've put it together perfectly. Daniel would be proud of you."

"I have to keep reminding myself of that Heather."

Merchandise was gathered as store assistants—even strangers complimented Annie. Plans were made to have the items delivered to the brownstone before seven, including Amish clothing now packed inside plastic bags. Explaining to Annie that everything would be written off as a business expense, Alicen noted the time.

"We don't want to be late." Still chattering, the three hurried out the door.

Handing Annie a pair of designer sunglasses, Alicen waited for reaction from males passing by. It didn't take long. In less than an hour after shedding her skin, Annie had become a magnet for male hormones. They'd never believe she was on her way to a spa/beauty salon for the first time in her life.

Being pampered left Annie a bit unsettled. Her hair had never been cut—just trimmed somewhat with sewing scissors, then pulled back and hidden. She declined a massage; not wanting to be touched by a stranger.

"We can add color and shine but it's her sense of self that makes the statement."

Such a description of Annie with gunk painted into her hair was spoken by the spa's owner; himself an interesting character. Recently marrying his girlfriend of 19 years, Artist Gregory as he preferred to be called, had been chosen style advisor for the President-elect. "It's an honor," he explained to anyone who'd listen, "She's what this country needs."

"Why do you like her?" Annie found politics fascinating.

"Her ability to simplify issues; that's what grabs me."

"Think that's because of her gender?"

"It's more her multicultural upbringing; that alone has allowed her a deeper understanding of humanity's frailties. Her contempt of special interests is an added plus. Troublesome will be the opposition she'll face."

"What do you mean?"

"Besides being a voice for the downtrodden, she's taking on the NGL. *That* is a dangerous road to travel."

"Guns are a way of life."

While shampooing Annie, Gregory explained.

"I accept the 2nd Amendment. But the hunting of innocent children and other victims is murder."

"Hunting children?"

"By lobbying against certain legislation, the NGL can delay or even defeat laws meant to protect the innocent."

Gregory continued. "There are too many guns made to do harm— not hunt wild game—on our streets. Caught in the cross hairs are the children. This is not the intention of our forefathers' words."

"Why would the NGL do that?"

"Power. It's all about power. Sit up honey."

His fingers worked through the wet hair. Annie likened it to kneading bread; the picking and brushing and snipping like adding eggs and flour to the mix. He then reached for a hairdryer. Back went those fingers, until each strand met his approval. After squeezing a dab of cream onto his hand, he rubbed his palms together; then applied the cream to Annie's hair. Snapping his fingers a young woman resembling a Barbie doll came and stood by his side, handing him what he demanded; turning Annie's face into that of a cover girl.

"What do you think, honey?" Artist Gregory had created another masterpiece.

Annie didn't recognize the person in the mirror. Her eyes seemed bigger. With cheekbones glowing and lips fuller, Annie had to get a closer look. She'd yet to notice the subtle line of accent in her hair or how it fell with a bit of a wave past her shoulders.

"It looks nice," Annie remarked, "but I could never do this every day. I'd always be late for work!"

"Oh my Sweetie," spouted Gregory, "You are so refreshing."

"Smashing," spoke a woman in the next chair over.

"We'll have a crash course on make-up tonight." Alicen knew all about make-up. Daniel often kidded she looked like a clown.

Collecting tubes and compacts and jars full of goo and sprays for frizz and pencils for accenting and shampoos for every mood and then putting it all on their account, Heather and Alicen were ready to find a restaurant.

But Annie had one more question of Gregory. "In whose interest is the NGL?"

"I repeat. Power is the driving force. Those who support the NGL reap the rewards of votes, favors—perks—and therefore, power. Strongly opposing the NGL played a role in electing this particular woman President. She speaks for other women who've walked a similar path."

'I don't understand."

"Our President-elect lost a child in a school shooting. Both shooters were armed with illegal assault weapons. That was the catalyst that began her journey to the White House."

Any woman who has lost a child would feel empathy thought Annie. It's a place no parent ever expects to be.

"Daniel's cousin lost a child in a school shooting. The man rushed in, lined the girls up and shot them in the head. Daniel and I often thought how frightened those children must have been. The girl's mother collapsed and died a few months later."

The salon became silent. It was Heather who spoke first.

"I'm famished. Gregory, you are amazing."

"I did nothing. This woman is a true beauty. I wish you well dearest Annie." Stepping closer, he whispered, "If we don't question, the world will never change."

"I agree," answered Annie. "We each have to do it our own way. Thank you for everything Gregory. I wish *you* the best in Washington."

"I thank you my darling. The President-elect is a real beauty herself—great cheek bones—that beautiful olive skin. I'm truly blessed to have been asked. Later!"

A long and leisurely lunch rolled close to the dinner hour. Then it was back to Heather's in preparation for the Saturday morning flight.

Philly

ATTEMPTING TO GET AS CLOSE TO Tommy's as he could, the cab driver passed Vine Street; then pulled to the curb and pointed. "Up there's your address."

Of all the historic structures standing in a row along the cobble-stone walkway, there was no guessing which place was Tommy's. He was sitting right there on the steps of a mustard-painted building with long windows. From a wrought iron pole hung a sign, "Studio of T.Catalano."

Heather rushed to give her friend a hug. Alicen followed. "It is so kind of you to take Annie under your wing," spoke Heather."

"I'm glad you asked."

Tommy didn't wait to be introduced. Holding out his hand he greeted his new roommate. "This must be Annie." He proceeded to tell her his place was her place.

Annie liked him instantly; sensing his sincerity spoken through blue eyes. He was a bit taller than Daniel. His wavy, almost black hair with a tad bit of grey was striking. His button-down was covered by a cranberry fleece; his jeans were worn. His boots the same. Such casualness made Annie feel welcomed.

"I thank you for providing me shelter."

"I'll help in any way I can. I am sorry for your loss Annie."

A sudden gust stirred the snow lying in heaps.

"Let's get inside."

Tommy helped with the luggage while Alicen paid the driver.

Once inside and through an archway painted a terra cotta with etchings representing the city's history mingling with long-stemmed wild flowers, Tommy explained.

"Many of the old timers don't like my blending history with the abstract; still others stop to take a picture."

"I've never been in an artist's studio," remarked Annie.

"It gets a little messy. Part of the process," he laughed, leading his guests past canvas and brushes and frames of every sort; then through his office complete with computer, printer, and a desk full of envelopes and paper stock.

"Home is this way."

Tommy continued down a hallway that opened into a living room complete with a fireplace. Another door opened.

"This will be your room Annie."

It was more than a bedroom. Included was a bathroom with a sunken tub and a closet capable of holding her new wardrobe and more. Window seats with pillows contrasting the deep lime walls overlooked the cobblestone pathway. The bed was a four poster; the dresser refinished with six ample drawers. After all the luggage was moved in, the tour continued.

"This is the kitchen—obviously. I love to cook; the reason for all the accessories."

Annie felt at home. It was the atmosphere; the old-looking yet modern oven; plank cupboards; the round oak pedestal table in the adjoining dining area surrounded by wainscoting. When he'd built their home, Daniel painstakingly made the wainscoting for the kitchen and front room. Daniel knew it would please Annie.

"My bedroom is through that hallway. Over there's a spare room with another computer. Feel free to log on whenever you please. I can't emphasize enough. Treat this as your home Annie. Come and go as you need. I'll give you a key."

No words could explain how Annie felt. No words were needed.

"I forgot to mention. Washer and dryer are behind that curtain."

"That's something I'll need help with."

Tommy thought for a moment.

"Looking at you, I forget you're Amish. No one at the paper will ever have a clue."

"Speaking of the paper Tommy?"

"Let Annie get settled first Heather."

Sensing there was something important about to be discussed Annie quickly unpacked while Tommy prepared a late lunch. Soon they were gathered around the table. The conversation came to a halt when Tommy turned to Annie.

"You have a job interview Tuesday, 9:30 at the Times Union."

"But how?"

"I collected on a favor."

"In the newsroom?"

"Yes. You'd be starting at the bottom but at least you'd be in the door."

"Who is the interview with?"

"One of the Morris family puppets."

"What do you mean?"

Refilling glasses, Tommy explained. "This is a dynasty of power; rooted back when newspapers ruled what the public heard—when they heard it—and how. That's all changed; first with cable; then with the internet. Now their headlines are old news. Even though most have versions of their print online, they've been hit by an economic downturn unlike any other. Cost of newsprint soaring; circulation down dramatically and a shrinking of advertising dollars generated both in classified and display—coupled with those new avenues of competition—have knocked newspapers out of the game. Many stalwart names in the business have ceased publishing. Their baby boomer customer base is growing older. Generations coming into play have been raised with the internet as their source of communicating and news gathering. No other print dynasty is more ruthless; more desperate to scoop the competition old and new than the Morris Publishing Group. Jack Morris Sr. has newsprint engrained under his fingernails. He's turned his papers into broadsheet tabloids printing whatever he pleases. He'll go to any length to remain #1. I mean—anything Annie. You are going into the fire."

It didn't take a second for Annie to reply.

"I've lost my child. In a sense, I've lost my husband. I know they are responsible. Call it a mother's instinct; something dark and evil is lurking. They pushed me into the fire the night my baby died in that cold, wet field and went home to our Lord."

The rest of the talk centered on Philadelphia. Tommy gave Annie a heads up on how things worked and who knew whom and who worked for and against whomever. He stressed the history of the city; how some wanted to use it to their own advantage while others tried desperately to preserve it for what it represented.

"One last thing Annie. You have to change your name. You've changed physically. You must do the same with your identity."

Leaving for a minute, Tommy returned with a manila envelope.

"In here is everything you'll need; birth certificate, social security card, resume, writing samples, and references. I'll get you on LinkedIn and Facebook. I'll keep you updated, online and in tune. You have to sell yourself as shrewd; make them believe you'll do anything for a scoop. Write anything demanded without reservation. They're not only ruthless. There are wolves amongst them out to prove their power in other ways. Do you understand what I mean by *anything?*"

"Although I travel by horse and buggy and cover myself from head to toe, I understand. The use of power for sex knows no discrimination. It happens in back fields as well as board rooms."

"With that understood, welcome to the asphalt jungle Annie Catalano—my long lost cousin from Boston."

Handing Annie the envelope, Tommy plugged the coffee pot in and prepared to serve dessert. Ironically upside down cake fit the moment.

The Interview

ANNIE'S REASON FOR WEARING THE TALL, black leather boots with narrow heels was the interview just 60 some minutes away. Heather and Alicen had returned to New York. Before leaving, Alicen again gave a demonstration on the art of hair and make-up.

Tommy was waiting in the kitchen with coffee ready—black with a touch of sugar.

"I like the hint of cleavage; good to play up your sexuality in that den of wolves. A turtleneck would have stated—boring. One look at you, and they'll remember the name with that face."

Judging by Tommy's response, Annie nailed the entire package. She'd put her hair up in a French twist; accessorized the black suit like an expert.

"I believe I have my new identity memorized. I went over the material yesterday—both at the hospital and after dinner. If I don't know Annie Catalano now, I never will."

Checking to make sure she had everything she might need, including a photo ID Tommy made through the help of a friend, Annie closed her portfolio.

"I am ready."

"You should be right on time. I'll have my phone on if you need me. Go get them Annie."

"Thanks for your help Tommy."

Hesitating for a moment, Annie stepped out into the city of brotherly love. A few minutes later she hailed a cab, unsure of where she really might be headed.

Turns out Tommy was right. Annie arrived in front of the imposing building with time to spare. The original part of the Morris building dated back to Washington's era. Located in the vicinity of Philly's historic district it was one of many tourist destinations. Some sought to take pictures while others hoped to catch a glimpse of Mr. Morris himself. The name alone was synonymous for breaking headlines from before the abolition of slavery straight on through.

Approaching the revolving door, Annie hesitated when catching a glimpse of her reflection in the glass. Quickly she hurried along as others were at her heels. Inside the lobby, people were going in all directions. One wall was sheer elevators; the opposite a sprawling reception desk over which hung a sign stopping Annie cold, "Morris Newspapers— The Jewel of Publishing" with that ruby logo staring down at her. Annie wanted to run or scream or beat the cold walls with her fists. Adding to her disgust was a fleet of those black cars with darkened windshields pulling up outside. Annie searched a freestanding directory of names and departments, then entered a waiting elevator.

"Hold it!" yelled a man in a long black coat running into the building. He was followed by more such men all piling into the elevator. Pushed to the back, Annie listened as talk centered around the playoffs—whether or not the Eagles would win the title.

"Great if they made it. Think of the papers we'd sell."

"If they lose we tear them down. That would sell even more. Bad news outsells good every time."

"Second floor" announced a recording. The door opened but no one moved. All those men turned around.

"Ladies first," spoke one as the rest moved aside.

Annie felt their eyes as her coat opened slightly; that hint of cleavage revealed. She didn't like their gawking at her like a piece of meat but then she had to remind herself where she was and why she was there.

"Excuse me," Annie said, brushing past the tallest man whose after shave about toppled her.

Off the elevator, she turned back around.

"Thank you gentlemen," she spoke, her chocolate eyes looking straight at them.

"Gentlemen. I like that," replied yet another as the bunch followed Annie, leaving her at the front desk. Annie watched as they walked into the newsroom, disappearing into the mass.

"May I help you?"

A somber woman, probably approaching her fifties Annie calculated, waited impatiently for a reply.

"Yes. I'm—I'm Annie Catalano. I have a 9:30 interview."

It would take awhile getting used to saying that she thought.

"Wait over there."

Returning shortly, the woman led Annie through the newsroom to an office with windows covered by blinds.

"You can wait in here."

After almost twenty minutes had passed, curiosity got the best of her. Annie walked over to where a picture of a young woman was framed alongside a degree from an Ivy League school. Other pictures were in a cluster.

"Those are my children if you are wondering. Annie. I'm Susan Morris. Thanks for coming in this morning."

"Morris" thought Annie. She must be one of *them*.

"Thank you. What beautiful children Mrs. Morris?" Annie extended her hand.

"Please, have a seat," the woman replied, shaking Annie's hand.

"Actually I'm single. I adopted the boys. I never could see myself married but I did want to be a mother and with so many children in need, I chose adoption."

Swallowing a lump in her throat, Annie replied, assuming her new identity to perfection.

"I would like to be a mother at some point. But right now. I'd prefer to put all my effort into writing for the Times Union."

"My grandfather would like that response. He brags to everyone how he's the oldest paper boy in Philadelphia. His father started him at the bottom and he's been here ever since. Let's get to it Annie."

And that they did. Susan Morris was impressed with Annie Catalano's honorary degrees—including BU and her experience at rival publications. Noting her journalism awards she complimented Annie on such in-depth reporting.

"Competition is stiff. I see you spent months with families in New Orleans. What a disaster that was."

"As soon as those levies broke and no one showed up to help I knew there'd be stories that had to be told."

"Disasters drive circulation. We need more of them and more often. Good for business—especially if you're the one breaking the story."

Pushing her chair back, she stood and approached Annie. "I'm impressed Annie. Grandfather preaches to go with the gut. We need someone right now. You'd be doing social items for a few weeks just so you can learn our style; then you'd be doing hard core reporting—your strength. I'll check your references. If I have a problem I'll give you a call but from what I see you're hired. It's that simple."

Annie didn't want to appear too desperate.

"Full-time?"

"Yes and most likely more than 40 hours; goes with working deadlines. Can't count the times we've pulled a story off the front page at press time for breaking news."

"I thrive on deadlines Miss Morris."

"Please, call me Susan. I sensed you had newspapers under your skin. Grandfather says you either have it or you don't. You have it."

The two women ironed out the details. It was decided that Annie would start in the morning.

"Let me give you a quick tour."

Back in the newsroom, Susan Morris continued. "This will be your computer; this—your file. Coffee's always on. Advertising is on the 4th floor; sports 3rd. The press of course is downstairs. I won't introduce you to everyone. You'd never remember them anyway. But this young man will be sitting next to you. Annie Catalano meet Carmen G. Rossi. He's been with us for about a year. Carmen comes from out west."

"Land of the Broncos—right Rossi?" yelled a fellow reporter.

"Right. Actually the southern tip of Italy but that goes back a few generations. Catalano? From where in Italy did your ancestors come?"

"I'm not sure. My parents divorced when I was two so I never knew my father's side of the family."

Annie wondered if she sounded convincing to this man about Daniel's height with a slight crew cut and wire-rimmed glasses. Carmen's next question was an easier one.

"So are you from Philly?"

"The Boston area."

"Land of the Red Soxs!" yelled that some reporter

"Yes. I've been to some games." Thanks to Tommy for that tidbit, thought Annie.

"When I think of Boston I think of the Boston Tea Party. History's the reason I moved to Philly. We're surrounded by it here. My father always said this is the place to write about history. I hope to make some."

"So you have your sights on writing some good stuff?"

"I do Ms. Catalano."

"Please. Call me Annie."

"I'd like to introduce you to some of the family," Susan interrupted.

"See you tomorrow Annie."

"It was a pleasure meeting you Carmen."

Weaving about computers and people on phones, the young Miss Morris waited for Annie; then opened a door.

"This is where headlines are thrashed out. Gets pretty rough in here. Wait just a second." Susan entered into what Annie could see was an impressive office overlooking nearby Independence Park. A faint odor of cigar came trickling out, sickening her. She'd smelled that the night her life changed forever. Telling herself to remain calm, she looked about, noting the long desk with leather chairs that about filled the room. Piles of old newspapers were stacked in corners. In the front was a chalkboard the same as in the one-room school house where she and Daniel sat side by side. Posted nearby were rival publications; even pubs from other countries. Plastered about were photos of what Annie concluded were generations of Morris'; many of them with dignitaries and leaders from around the world, Presidents, sports legends; even some Hollywood stars. Many were signed. AP Awards and civil recognitions were mingled amongst the faces.

It was the gruffness in a voice laughing while entering the room that Annie recognized, sending tingles down her spine. That was the laugh that kept her up at night.

"I'd like you to meet some of the team." Susan brought Annie back off old Co. Rt. 68. "This is my father—Teddy Morris; my uncle Stephen Morris—all on the board and all editorial contributors. My cousin Joseph Morris is head of advertising. My brother Willie Morris is the Sports Editor—and this is my grandfather—Jack Morris. You have a lot of newsprint in this room."

Jack Morris spoke for the family.

"Welcome to Morris Publishing, Miss Catalano. Susan tells me how impressed she is with you. She's shared with us your understanding the vital role print has played and will continue to play in this country. Nothing will overtake this medium. Nothing."

"I agree Mr. Morris. I thank you for this opportunity."

That was it; short and sweet. There were stories to be written and leads to follow.

Annie was to be at work at 8 a.m.

Riding the elevator down to the lobby, her mind was racing. Which one of those men was the drunken driver responsible for Jacob's death?

That sickening laugh had haunted her. She'd played it over and over in her mind many nights when lying in wait of dawn. I have no children; not anymore that is, Miss Morris, she wanted to scream. One of your blood relatives is responsible for my baby's death.

Fresh air was what Annie needed. Hailing a cab she headed back to Tommy's. After changing, she'd call Heather; then spend the day with Daniel.

The Rat Race

THE SOCIAL ITEM THING LASTED SHORT of a week. Now three weeks into it, Annie had established some sort of a routine—unless headlines had to be changed and the lead replaced. Daniel had a slight setback so surgery was pending. Annie periodically sent word back to the Bishop to keep him at bay. Knowing Daniel was receiving the best of care gave Annie the strength she needed to be swallowed up in the rat race. She checked in with his nurse about lunchtime every day. If she wasn't working she'd sit with him in the evening until they were ready to prep him for the night. Once they phoned at 7 in the morning, telling Annie he'd called her name out just before dawn. Annie was late for work that day.

She didn't mind working evenings—except for one in particular. She was having a hard time wrapping up a story. It'd been assigned by Susan Morris who wanted it in the morning paper. Her problem had nothing to do with a lack of material. It had everything to do with one of the Morris men staying late. The only thing he was working on was trying to get into Annie's pants as Carmen described the obnoxious man's advances. After Annie finally filed her story and was on her way out, Stephen Morris was at the elevator waiting for her. This cat and mouse thing was something foreign to Annie. Daniel had been the love of her life since she was twelve. He never forced himself on her. He never made small talk to impress her; nor did he slick back his hair or wear gold

71

chains. Daniel didn't have to do any of that. Just his very presence spoke of a man secure in who he was, what he wanted, and where he came from. Annie was becoming increasingly aware of the latter; realizing what an upbringing such as theirs had instilled in them even though she fought it all the way. This Mr. Morris was the opposite. He *was* a Morris. So after small talk and a few laughs, he'd asked her to go for a drink at his place. Annie tried the headache thing but it didn't work so when the elevator door opened she pulled another excuse.

"Go ahead Mr. Morris. I just remembered something."

He didn't budge.

"Okay Mr. Morris," Annie said, entering the elevator and in a hurry, pushed the main lobby button. "I can play too."

"Please call me Steve. You make me feel old when you call me Mr. Morris."

"I was raised to respect my elders."

"With age comes experience. You know what I'm talking about Annie?"

"I was also raised not to have sex with my boss."

"You do get to the point. I see that in your writing. Crisp. Factual. That's a real turn on."

The door opened but it didn't matter. The lobby was about empty.

"Since you cut to the core Miss Annie, let's forget the drinks. Sex with one's boss could be a real turn on for the both of us." Getting closer, he wrapped his arm around Annie's waist. "However you want it, this experienced boss can give it." With his other hand he pulled away Annie's silk blouse and brought his lips to hers.

That's when she kneed him.

"Your kind of experience I don't need Mr. Morris. I have enough of my own."

With that she walked slowly but surely out of the building. The next day a dozen roses awaited her—the card reading:

"I haven't been kneed like that in a long time."

From then on, Steve Morris was on her "avoid-at-all-costs-list."

Carmen became like an older brother to Annie. Although she grew up with several brothers she felt closer to this stranger who'd taken her under his wing. If they were lucky to have time for lunch Carmen would take Annie on walking tours. She had so many questions. Carmen knew the answers.

"My father's ancestors came to Ellis Island with only their clothes on their backs. They had a vision of what they wanted and this was the country that made it possible. Both my parents teach American History so that's always been the dinner conversation. I'm an only child. I absorbed it all. My father especially is a scholar on the Declaration. He attributes all of his success to the guiding principles drawn out over two hundred years ago. Fascinating is that what our forefathers wrote still rings true. From the Liberty Bell to Constitution Hall we are surrounded by the foundation of this country Annie!"

Listening to Carmen, Annie wanted to tell him her story. Tommy told her to wait; that it was too early in the game. She couldn't trust any of them. Maybe Carmen was playing games too.

The last week in January brought grimmer revenue reports. They tried everything to build ad lineage—both on and offline. Even though the Morris family did not support the new President, they understood the meaning of her inauguration; printing extra copies of a commemorative edition jammed pack with congratulatory advertising. They sold out within hours. They revamped their Sunday Art Section featuring more in-depth stories on artists in Old City. The article receiving the best response was that of Tommy and his arch. It also caused a buzz in the newsroom. The word was out. Acclaimed artist T. Catalano was Annie's cousin.

But the real writing was on the wall. Jack Morris felt his dynasty crumbling. Through conference calls he'd rant, telling reporters to get out there; use all their connections; dig for those scoops by whatever means they felt necessary. He wanted breaking headlines. He'd settle for nothing less. He'd take no excuses. Such outrage was the reason for high employee turnover. Surprising to Annie—Susan Morris was even more demanding.

Taking advantage of having a Saturday off, Annie spent the morning with Daniel. Doctors were encouraged. Surgery was scheduled for

Tuesday. Annie called Tommy to tell him the news. Tommy himself had just hung up the phone with a major art magazine who wanted to do a spread on his studio.

"What a day for good news! When you return Annie, I want to take you to some place special."

With Daniel resting comfortably, Annie headed back to Tommy's. He was waiting for her. Seconds later they were in a cab.

The snow was coming down a little harder as the driver pulled up to the curb.

"Welcome to one of the hottest spots in town Annie—even in late January."

A sign told the surprise—Reading Terminal Market. Carmen talked about the market all the time.

It was amazing with everything from ethnic food to jewelry and flowers. Amish were everywhere. Some were selling baked goods; others jars of jam and pickles. Wicker baskets were displayed with quilts and pillows. The furniture really caused a stir. While most were drawn to the craftsmanship, it was the smells that drew Annie in; varnish mingling with fresh breads and homemade pies. A young boy asked Annie if she wanted anything. Taken back by his Buster Brown haircut and wide-brimmed hat, Annie felt her heart quicken. She bought four bags of cookies; then asked if he himself would like one of the molasses ones. They were Jacob's favorites. They appeared to be his too!

"Did you bake these?"

The young woman tending to the boy smiled, nodding yes.

"Are you from around here?"

"Cedar Flats. We own over a hundred acres."

Annie stayed, talking to the Amish girl. The longer she did the more she realized Cedar Flats was where Daniel's family member was killed in a school shooting. She wanted to tell her about Daniel and Jacob and how she made the same cookies she was now eating but she didn't.

"Is this your little boy?"

"Yes."

"What's his name?"

"Jonah. He was a twin."

"Twin! Twin boys? Girls?"

"He had a twin sister," the young mother hesitated. "But she was shot and died shortly afterwards."

Annie had a feeling. She didn't go there.

"I lost a child. I understand."

"We are to forgive. I say the Lord's Prayer. It helps me to follow our teachings."

"I say the Lord's Prayer too but haven't been able to forgive. I believe in the teachings but my child's death was unnecessary."

"That's when you trust in the Lord."

"I do. I trust in the Lord. I trust He will lead me to those responsible."

Keeping her head down, the young woman whispered, "I saw the man's picture in the paper; the man responsible for the shooting of my child—and I," she moved closer, "I saw the devil. I can say no more." For some reason the Amish mother felt she could tell her deepest feelings to this stranger.

Annie understood the importance of this moment. Admitting and then speaking such thoughts was taboo. Although wanting to dig deeper, Annie did not want to frighten her. "Losing a child in such a senseless tragedy is impossible to put into words, let alone accept." That was the extent of it.

Changing the subject Annie asked, "What's your name?"

"Emily. And yours?"

"Annie—Annie Finley. I work downtown. It's nice to meet you Emily."

The two talked while Jonah sold baked goods. Other Amish women joined in the conversation. They were drawn to Annie. When Tommy came looking for Annie, Emily told her she was at the market every week, Thursday through Saturday. She hoped to talk with Annie again.

"I'll be back," she told Emily. "We'll continue where we left off."

Saying good-bye to the others and shaking Jonah's hand, Annie went to see what Tommy was watching.

"Some sort of a protest Annie."

A few of the dissenters came inside; following them was Carmen.

"Carmen. This is your Saturday on desk. Why are you here?"

"Old man Morris sent me."

After exchanging a few pleasantries with Tommy, Carmen explained. "I was on the phone when Morris came bursting into the newsroom. He'd just read a White House announcement over the wire saying the President will be coming to Philly to roll out her push to amend the 2nd Amendment. When that news hit, gun lovers called for a show of protest. That's what you're seeing. I can only imagine how great the dissent will be once she finally gets here. Bet it will be larger than back in '03. The NGL immediately put a press release out encouraging gun owners around the country to show up and stand together that day. They even called Morris personally."

"When is the President coming?" Tommy found the thought of her visit intriguing.

"Middle or late February. She's to give a speech on the steps of Independence Hall. Imagine that—the very spot where the Declaration of Independence was debated and adopted. She's gutsy for sure. Morris will be holding strategy sessions starting Monday. He's out to sell papers anyway he can. It's going to get dirty."

"What do you mean?"

"These are two powerful opposing sides coming together where those principles I told you about were written. One is out to defend the Constitution. The other wants to change it. What a story—however you slant it. And if you're in Morris' shoes it could put you back on top. That's why we have to be in his office 8 am Monday. He'll get breaking headlines out of us however he can."

"But we do that every day?"

"He's been given the gift of a huge news event right in his backyard. If somehow it could be even bigger, look at the papers he'll sell."

"Why do people object to better controlling gun criminals?" This issue seemed to be following Annie. She had to ask.

"The Second Amendment states our right to bear arms."

"Hunting on streets and in schools and shopping malls is not what they had in mind."

"The right to bear arms is part of our Constitution."

"Circumstances change. We don't hunt for survival. The death of one child through gun violence is one too many."

"You're on the liberal side Annie."

"She's on the side of mothers."

It was Emily speaking out. No one was more shocked than Annie. No one understood more than Annie how significant the moment was.

"I better cover the story before I'm part of it." Wrapping a scarf around his neck, Carmen headed back out the door. "Remember what Washington said ladies—*"Firearms are second only to the Constitution in importance; they are the peoples' liberty's teeth—"*

"I'll see you Monday Annie."

His parents would be proud of him was all Annie could think as Carmen disappeared into the mass. All that dinner conversation had sunk in.

"I did not intend to listen or interrupt but something overcame me. I pray it was not the devil. I pray for your forgiveness Annie."

"It was not the devil Emily. It was because you are a mother and that does not beg anyone's forgiveness. You lost a child. A mother is a mother, Emily, no matter where or how she lives."

"You are a special woman Annie. I must go."

Turning back around Emily asked, "Do you work with this reporter? He said he'd see you Monday."

"No. We go to the same gym. That's where we argue policies."

Annie was getting good at covering her tail. She had to—for now.

Back at the studio, Tommy cooked some chicken stir fry while Annie talked with Heather and Alicen who were back out on the road. It was Alicen who told Annie they were almost side swept by one of those black shiny cars in her neck of the woods. She also told Annie that her sister Mary was expecting a baby.

How ironic, thought Annie later that evening while lying in bed, some have too many children while others have theirs taken away. It was a single star that caught her attention. *"Good night to you too my sweet boy."* As her thoughts turned to Carmen's departing words she fell asleep, aware the Lord had more than one reason for her presence in this city of stature by the Delaware

Monday's Meeting

IT WAS THE FIRST TIME ANNIE had been in *the* office. Judging from photos of Jack Morris standing proudly next to dead carcasses from around the world his stand on the 2nd Amendment needed no clarification. Noticing her eyeing the pictures he took the opportunity to boast.

"Do you do much hunting in Boston, Ms. Catalano? I see you're drawn to my trophy excursions."

"My family hunts. I too have shot a gun."

"And what have they hunted?"

"Deer, geese, some rabbit."

"That's really not hunting. You need to go after the big game. Such a rush I can't explain," Walking to the photos, he continued. "This was in Africa; this Alaska; this Saskatchewan; this Utah or Montana. This I can't even remember. I've been all around the world. Hunting is a sport of the true man."

Carmen had warned Annie before heading into the meeting.

"Don't even go there with your liberal views. You'll be surrounded by gun lovers. You don't want to be marked as anything but a gun touting lover."

"You should see his study. Heads mounted all over the walls," laughed Susan Morris. She was joined in by everyone else. Annie tried but she couldn't muster a smile. As they went on, her eyes fell upon a series of plaques arranged by year awarded to the Morris Publishing Group. They were in recognition of their allegiance to the National Gun Lobby. Some were distinguished awards, singling out Jack Morris for support of that organization through editorials; some for private donations. Looking at those, then looking around the room, the realization of what Carmen said sunk in. She was surrounded by those who believed in the core of that amendment no matter what the hunt.

"Help yourselves to coffee. This is the first strategy session in preparation of the new President's stop in our city. I needn't go on about how I feel about her. Not because she's a woman—let me get that straight. Don't want to be accused of being anti-gender or racial or anything like that when it comes to the highest office in our land but for her, or anyone, to even question our fundamental Bill of Rights written by wise and fair men over two hundred years ago, that baffles me. It's incomprehensible. They should write a law about that while they're spouting off—making something out of nothing. The right to bear arms is a fundamental principle of this democracy. We must do everything in our power to defeat this woman. How dare she use our city—this country's first national capital—as her platform to tout change to our Bill of Rights. She will be sorry she ever stepped into where the history of our nation is embedded."

The Morris family clapped; truly moved by the words of their leader. Carmen and others joined in. Annie went for coffee.

"Here's my plan. Remember—what is discussed here stays here. There are consequences. Understand?"

After a short silence, he continued. "It's simple. We bring her down even before she gets here. That's where you come in Ms. Catalano. Besides being female, you have hunting in your genes, although limited. I want you to research this woman. Dig deep. Find me whatever you can. We need to discredit her. If you can't find anything, fabricate it. We'll back you all the way. We have to plant seeds of doubt and mistrust in the minds of our readers. The stupid fools will do the rest.

It happens every time. Just look back at history. Throw them some meat and they'll attack like piranhas. That's the way freedom of the press works."

Carmen spoke up. "I'd like to assist Annie. Time is limited. I believe if we worked as a team, we can create a stronger package."

"Good idea Rossi. Background is left to you two eager beavers. You're the history buff so that will free Catalano up to go for the throat."

"I understand what you're after Mr. Morris." Annie felt her stomach churn as the others thought she was part of this lynching. She felt Steve Morris' eyes staring at her. She knew what that Mr. Morris wanted.

"Any questions Ms. Catalano—Susan or Steve can help."

His help would be nailing her wherever and whenever he could. If you only knew Jack Morris Annie thought, sitting there in a boardroom full of mindless executives. But then, he probably did.

"All of our papers will be used in this campaign. We will start pushing our agenda immediately. Dig in the archives. I need features on this issue. Others have tried to defeat the 2nd but this is different. This could be the nail in the coffin. You're a history buff Rossi. I want articles on this City's heritage; profiles on the framers of our democracy. Quote them. Make it up if you have to. None of them are able to sue me. Interview those supporting our stand. This city is full of radical 2nd Amendment lovers. Prepare to stay late and put out—or get out. And when she gets here, I want her covered every second of the way."

"I remember Washington saying—*The very atmosphere of firearms anywhere and everywhere restrains evil interference—they deserve a place of honor with all that's good.*"

"Great quote Rossi. That's what I'm talking about. Email that to Catalano. Starting off with our first President setting the tone is a comparison worth noting. It provides us the moral authority to follow in his footsteps. We have papers to publish. Go to work—all of you!"

"Annie. I need to speak with you—now."

It was apparent something was bothering Susan as she rushed out of the room.

Reaching her office, she waited for Annie; then shut the door.

Looking out upon the park, she spoke in a tone Annie had not heard until now.

"You're not a gun lover are you? I saw it in your expressions as my grandfather was speaking. You don't believe in anything he said, do you? You probably think this lady President is good for this country; probably agree she'll get those horrible guns out of the hands of criminals; probably think we don't have the right to bear arms, do you? Well let me tell you something—you best keep those thoughts to yourself if you know what I mean. Get out there and get the dirt he wants. And if you don't think you can do that then pack it up. Your kind comes a dime a dozen. You win a few awards and you think you can go rogue. Well not here. Toe the line or get to hell out. We have papers to sell and damn it that is what we are going to do. We are the jewel of publishing because we go after it and crush the competition every time. We break the news. We create the news. Understand?"

"Understand. No matter what my personal opinions are my allegiance is to this paper Miss Morris."

"Don't even give my grandfather a reason to think otherwise. Women pick up on other women's emotions. There is something going on below the surface with you, Catalano, that I cannot pinpoint. Remember this, I will be watching you and if anything shows me a red flag I'm pulling your cover. Nothing and no one can jeopardize Morris Publications. We remain on top and we will stay on top with or without you on board. This is our story and we will shape it however we feel necessary. The environment we are in demands loyalty. Jump through the hoops and give him what he wants or get out."

"I'm on board Miss Morris."

"One more thing; don't flatter yourself by Steve's attention. He goes after anything in a skirt. He'd prefer to be taking the skirt off."

"I figured that out awhile back."

"Get to work—and email me everything you send to Jack separately."

"Separately?"

"Yes. Do you have a problem with that?"

"No. Whatever you say."

"We never had this conversation Catalano. Maybe if you had children you'd understand what it means to put others needs ahead of your own. I've worked too hard to have someone outside the family screw an opportunity of a lifetime."

"We never had this conversation."

With that, Annie shut the door; anger building almost to the tipping point. Calm down she told herself. This heartless woman is consumed in greed. She has no clue of how to put others ahead of her own lust for power. Those poor adopted children were probably better off before she swooped across the ocean and snatched them up. Artist Gregory was right. The quest for power can destroy. Her cell phone ringing brought her back to the moment.

It was the hospital. Daniel was awake. He was asking for her—and Jacob.

Daniel

"BAD NEWS ANNIE? YOU LOOK SHOCKED."

Before she could get her bearings; before she could even answer Carmen, her name was being shouted over the intercom.

"Annie Catalano. Line three."

"I'll take it Annie."

While Carmen answered questions about setting up an interview, Annie had all she could do to hold back tears as she sat amongst those who caused them. Swirling through her mind were those headlights flashing and the horse bucking; the image of Daniel laying on that wet road and her baby lifeless in the field. A part of her wanted to rush to Daniel's side; part of her wanted to crawl into a corner. How could she do this? How could she walk into that hospital room and tell Daniel their precious Jacob was dead. She'd thought about this moment every day since that November night. But every time the thoughts came, she put it off until tomorrow.

Tomorrow had turned into today with a single phone call. The moment was here. She had to put aside her fears; find strength for the both of them. They'd always been there for each other. This would be their greatest test.

"You're not listening Annie. You're white as a ghost. What has happened?"

"I need to leave. You have to cover for me Carmen without asking questions."

"Go do what you have to do. Don't worry about this place. I'll start researching."

Annie didn't care about the President or any of the Morris'. She had to get to the hospital.

"Take this. It will look like you're going on assignment. Call or text if you need me."

Handing her a notebook and camera, he told her to leave.

Upon arriving at the hospital and heading to the elevator is when Annie remembered she couldn't go into Daniel's room wearing her ivory, tight-fitting sweater dress. She had to find Pauline.

"I'm looking for Pauline." The woman in the gift shop kept sorting cards in the rack.

"It's her day off."

Afraid she'd not be able to go to Daniel, she asked in urgency, "Is there a young man working today—with a pleasant smile and possibly wearing a bow tie. I can't remember his name but if he is here I must talk to him."

"That would be Todd. I'll get him."

"Please Lord. Please let it be Todd."

Her prayer was answered. Pleasant smiling Todd was there and he remembered her—even though she now looked like one of the models on a nearby magazine cover.

"Pauline told me I was not to ask questions. Just help you in any way I can."

"You already have."

"I'll make sure no one goes out back while you're getting changed."

"Thank you Todd. Thank you so much."

Shutting the door, Annie promptly pulled the dress over her head and kicked off her heels. With a sink and mirror nearby make-up was removed; hair brushed; then pulled back and up. There were all the straight pins and bobby pins she might need. The boots were her exact size. She never thought she'd miss wearing them but after spiked heels the boots were a welcomed relief. Taking a last look before stepping back out into the world as Annie Finley, she noticed a trace of eye make-up that needed removing. That's when she heard Todd speaking with another employee.

"No need to check the backroom now. I'll get the ladder and bring it to you."

Making sure her bonnet was secure and all make-up had disappeared, Annie passed through the bookstore, nodding to Todd as she exited. Waiting for the elevator she noticed an honor box full of newspapers. One of the lead stories was written by an Annie Catalano.

"Mr. Finley opened his eyes a little after seven this morning. It was as if he knew his surgery was tomorrow and he had something to say about it."

"What *did* he say? Does he have any idea of where he is or why he's here?"

"We told him nothing. All he has asked is where his family is. We've kept telling him you'd be here soon. Take all the time you need."

His eyes were closed as Annie approached the bed. Many of the tubes had been removed. Annie had signed a paper giving permission to have Daniel's beard shaved—mandatory for surgery. He'd had the beard since they were married so it was like looking at someone she knew a long time ago. Some used to say Jacob looked like her but now, as Daniel lay against the white sheet and the beard was gone it was as if Annie was looking at an older version of Jacob. That's when Daniel opened his eyes.

"Annie—my Annie."

"I've missed you my love."

"Sit by me. Tell me what the sorrow in your eyes is saying."

He sensed their loss even before she spoke. As Annie sat down and held both his hands in hers, she told him what had happened that dreadful night on old Co. Rt. 68.

"Jacob's buried in the back of the cemetery under the apple tree with his blanket and favorite book. You know how he loved the apple orchard Daniel. Bear is at home—on his bed. I needed something to hold on to."

"I wish I could have been there to hold you Annie."

"You were Daniel. You were there."

"We were blessed with an angel my dearest wife. We were truly blessed."

As snowflakes kept falling along with tears of great sadness, Annie told Daniel everything. She hadn't realized how much she missed having his attention. She held nothing back. Daniel was supportive of her every move.

"I have a cell phone Daniel. If you need me the nurses know my number. I can be here in an instant. Don't worry about me. We need you to get through the surgery."

"Please stay safe. I'm with you my every step of the way as is our little Jacob. Your strength gives me strength."

"We *were* blessed Daniel. We were truly blessed."

She could have sat by his bedside all day. But she realized Annie Catalano had a full plate back at the office. Before leaving she spoke with the doctors. Everyone was optimistic about the surgery. Awake and alert now, Daniel's vitals were stronger than ever. Surgery was scheduled for 9 a.m. If all went as planned, Daniel could be on his feet sometime the end of the week. Annie would be either at the hospital or on the phone with his nurses.

With her mind full she stepped onto the elevator not noticing a man standing next to her. It was that disgusting cigar odor that jolted her into the present. Surely the Morris' were not the only ones smoking that revolting brand. It couldn't be. She'd just left all of them plotting the downfall of a President.

The elevator stopped on the floor below. In stepped two men. Annie moved to the back. With her head down; her face partially hidden by her bonnet she peered to her left. Yes. Oh my God Yes! It was Steve Morris. Right there next to her on this elevator going down to the lobby. She turned toward the wall, hiding her face completely.

"What are you reporting on today Morris?" asked a bald-headed man with thick glasses.

"An accident. Some drunk lost control of his SUV and almost hit some kids on their way to school."

"Thought you had string reporters covering the mundane," replied the other man engrossed in doing a crossword puzzle. "Last I heard you gave up chasing sirens for skirts!"

"You two are radio men; in advertising sales no less. That explains your ignorance. With the nature of news today, mountains can be made out of mole hills if you know what I mean. Turns out this guy is married to the President of the School Board. What a gift horse. Hammer the point away that the lady's husband is a drunk. Even worse, he jeopardized the very school safety she lectures about and bingo—we rid that Board of the liberal lady. It's a done deal. People will vote her out without even thinking."

"You guys in print. You look more like a tabloid than a newspaper these days! You're all crazy. I'll stick to CNN." The two departed when the elevator stopped on the 3rd floor.

"Getting off—Miss?"

Annie shook her head no.

Steve Morris moved a little closer as the door slid shut. "Going down to the main floor?"

Clearing her throat, Annie replied, "Yes."

"From around here?" Pushing the button for the lobby, Morris was now right next to her.

"Yes."

With his shoulder touching hers he kept at her. "You know the Amish have always intrigued me," his hand was now creeping underneath her cloak. She kept her face hidden as the elevator stopped on the 2nd floor. With no one waiting to get on, Annie knew she had to make a move. But this time she was in such a hurry her knee missed her target.

The blow was enough to startle him. Running out of the elevator her bonnet pushed back slightly as he looked up at her, startled by the incident.

Annie rushed through a doorway and down the stairs. Around she went passed the 1ˢᵗ floor and down more stairs to the lobby. She heard him coming. He seemed to be skipping steps. She felt his breath. How far behind he was she didn't know but Annie realized she had to keep going. Through the door she went, flying into the gift shop, passed Todd and into her little room, slamming the door shut. Annie waited in silence. She thought she might vomit but she stood, shaking, reciting the Lord's Prayer and calling on Jacob to stay by her side.

"Have you seen an Amish woman rush in here? I think she's unstable and in need of attention." Steve Morris slowed his pace; caught his breath and began searching the aisles.

"No I haven't sir," replied Todd all cool and calm. "But if I do I will alert security should I feel it necessary."

"Mind if I look around? I'm with the Times Union. Wouldn't want anyone to be at risk."

"Go right ahead. Feel free. But as I said, I've noticed nothing unusual."

While pretending to work on a display behind the counter, Todd kept an eye on Morris through mirrors on the ceiling.

"What's through there?"

"Just storage. I've been right here all morning. I haven't seen anything out of the ordinary."

"I'll take a quick look."

Annie heard their conversation. She sensed him getting closer. That's when she remembered Carmen's parting words, "Call or text me."

So she did, telling him to call Steve Morris on his cell immediately. Tell him anything. Just get him back at the paper.

Instantly Morris' phone rang inches from where Annie was hiding. His hand was on the doorknob.

"Hey Carmen. What to hell you calling me for? I know deadlines. Be right in." He stopped talking but was he still there? Annie sensed he was lingering. That cigar stench was about to make her sick.

"Hey kid. What's in here?" He was turning the knob.

"You have no authority to be searching this area." It was Pauline; right outside the door with Morris. "I must ask you to leave or I will report you for trespassing. Surely you have bigger stories to fill your pages—or do you?"

That angered Steve Morris. No one talked to a Morris like that.

"I have stories bigger than this rinky dink facility. Some stories might even make you blush. I could make you blush."

"Don't even try buster," laughed Pauline. "It takes a bigger man than you to make me blush—like my husband. I suggest you leave."

With that parting shot, he did.

By the time Pauline opened the small closet, Annie had her sweater dress on; hair down and heels on.

"That was a close one honey. You okay? You look a little peaked."

"Nothing make-up can't hide. Thanks for saving me Pauline."

"It was my pleasure. I can't stand any of that clan. It did my heart good to put him in his place. Their days of ruling this city are over."

"That's the hope for sure. Now I have to beat him back to the office."

"Let me get you a cab."

Thanking Todd, Annie followed Pauline, already outside in the circle. Waving her hands at one particular cabby she slipped him more than enough cash, telling him to get her friend to the Union building in ten minutes or she'd find him and get her money back.

Annie was there in less than eight minutes; at her desk in nine. About fifteen minutes later Steve Morris came rushing in. Annie smelled him nearby but never looked up; pretending to be engrossed in a conversation with Carmen.

Seemingly satisfied that it was a coincidence the Amish woman kneed him as Annie Catalano had done, he hurried into his office. Deadlines were approaching.

"Thanks Carmen. You saved me."

"I won't ask any questions. When you are ready I am here to listen."

"It's about family, Carmen. Gets complicated."

"Families are complicated. I more than understand."

The remainder of the day was spent on trying to dig up dirt on the President. It was a hard thing to do. She was clean as a whistle—rare for a politician.

Building the Case

TWO WEEKS HAD PASSED. DANIEL'S SURGERY was proving to have been successful. Much had happened at the paper and still so much lay ahead. Under the microscope of Jack Morris, the team of Catalano and Rossi mastered the art of planting innuendos in each feature written. Annie made certain to send Susan everything before it ran. Their bylines were getting attention. Their inboxes were full of reader comments. Most were favorable. Editors were shrewd with placement, making certain not to bury their features on an inside page. Op-Eds written by some big names backed up the articles. Readers were manipulated into thinking they had to get out and rally in defense of their right to bear arms even if they had no opinion on the issue. Annie was playing her role to the hilt, while despising every lie printed.

"Time for the kill?"

"The kill! I thought that's what we've been doing?"

It was at the end of one of those daily morning bashings with Jack Morris. Annie had come to realize the old news man respected those who spoke up. Puppets were a dime a dozen.

"The kill Catalano. You and Rossi have built your case. President Romero is a *foreigner*. You've pounded that one-word description of her over and over. When she comes riding into town attempting to rewrite history she will be perceived as an outsider. Keep building your case.

We've come down to the wire. We'll continue to spin whatever you write. What to hell we'll put it on milk cartons if need be. I don't give a damn how we do it. We need the final nail in her coffin. Papers are selling like hotcakes. Keep it up!"

Annie and Carmen had reignited old questions concerning the President's citizenship and her father's possible ties to Puerto Rican rebels. Doubts had been raised before as to whether or not she was qualified to run. Hammered out in debates and slung consistently by the other side right up to Election Day, the goal was to paint her as some sort of alien. Experts on U.S. Law agreed that although born in Puerto Rico, her mother being a US citizen who'd lived a few years in the States when she and her Puerto Rican husband were having problems, qualified Isabel as a natural born citizen. In politics, repeated accusations most often become accepted truths. But this year, that strategy backfired. Fed up with mudslinging, old-time dirty politics, Isabel Romero was seen as a fresh, educated voice with a keen ability to listen; able to digest complex issues and then make her decision. She didn't shy away from controversy. She tackled it. Of course the fact that her only child had been gunned down in that school shooting won her both sympathy and support from both sides and both genders. Gun violence was at an all-time high. President Romero was out to stop it.

She first came to the U.S. as a freshman at Princeton. Romero loved the States; proving herself every step of the way up to the very top. She married a Puerto Rican—her first love from grade school. A successful businessman, he spent his time between the States and Puerto Rico.

Choosing Pennsylvania as the kick-off state for her anti-gun campaign was jumping right into the fire and Catalano/Rossi reignited the flames. Although Romero had won Pennsylvania in the election, she'd alienated the huge block of NGL supporters. Gun laws were anything but strict in PA. The State Appeals Court had thrown out Philadelphia's ordinances to both limit gun purchases to one a month and ban assault weapons.

As Carmen explained, "Philly's become a weapons source for criminals in New York and other states with stricter gun laws."

Illegal trafficking of guns was big business. That and gun sales had more than doubled since it was evident Isabel Romero was a strong contender for the oval office. There was a showdown coming in historic Philly.

"So what do we do for a finale?"

On the surface Annie appeared desperate to scrape up more bait and sell more papers. That was the obvious reason; underneath the facade was her hope of being confided in by the Morris family. Although Susan never praised Annie, she hadn't criticized her since that confrontation in her office. Annie felt she'd appeased the woman—for now at least.

"I remember when things were heating up last October. Photos circulating the internet showed Romero—before she entered Princeton—at a gathering of her father's clan. Some standing in the background were holding rifles. The opposition tried to make a link between her anti-gun stance and her own family's use of guns or even that her father was some sort of an outlaw. In the end, none of it stuck thanks to her efficiently run campaign. If I could find the photos, I might be able to do a little magic."

"Like what?"

"Get me a coffee Annie and watch the master."

A genius with the computer, Carmen went in and had the photos on the screen before Annie returned.

"Look at these. Give me a minute."

And that's all it took. By cutting and pasting and snipping here and there young Isabel Romero was standing tall and beautiful—proudly holding on to a rifle; surrounded by Puerto Rican army types with guns and ammo criss-crossing their chests and hers.

"Could these soldiers have been rebels?"

"We can paint them as rebels Carmen! Gun-toting rebels in Puerto Rico. All the Morris' will love it. Print that photo!"

"You know there will be accusations Annie. The White House will put out a press release stating the photo has been altered."

"And you know what Jack Morris will say—plant that seed of doubt and the rest will take care of itself. I say we go for it. This is the nail old Jack wanted. This will keep the presses running overtime."

"You're beginning to sound just like him."

"Just doing my job."

"I heard the Secret Service is reading everything we write. They've been in town for weeks. Security will be unprecedented."

"As you've told me more than once, what she is trying to do is unprecedented."

"True. It's being watched all around the country. My father emailed me, telling me he and my mother are coming to Philly. Being such constitutional scholars, they're appalled that the President of the United States would dare question the words of our founders. He feels somehow she should be stopped."

"Think she'll succeed?"

"I fear in the long run she might. Although the NGL is teeming in power and influence the people are behind her. Looking back at history, when the people speak, change happens. Her election alone was that voice being heard. Although the President wouldn't be involved in the actual process, her opinion and weight can put pressure on Congress and the states. Get the right mix in those positions and yes—it could happen."

"Between the two of us, why is saving children wrong?"

"So you're back to that, you Liberal?"

"I'm just asking. I hate labels Carmen. Liberal or Conservative; Democrat or Republican—we're all Americans."

"You live in a country where labels are how we are identified even if they're not true. The newspaper prints labels every day. And remember, there is a stark difference in ideology and approach to issues between the two parties."

"Labels or no labels, we all should be on the side of saving children."

"Why the liberal streak? Where does it come from?"

"It's not a liberal thing. It's our duty to protect the innocent. Now please process the photo. Then we'll get writing."

Two hours later, with another Catalano/Rossi feature and that manipulated photo in his hands, Jack Morris called a meeting.

"They've nailed one hell of a piece. I want a spread in tomorrow's editions on the front page. Great work on the photo Rossi. From an anonymous source—right? Only has to be out there once. John Q.

Average American will do the rest—brainless souls that they are. It's our job to tell them what to believe. One week to go before Romero shows up. This will throw the dirt on her coffin."

Even Susan Morris praised the two for exceptional reporting. She was so pleased that she invited them to her grandfather's annual Valentine Ball that Saturday night. It was the event of the year; a gathering of the elite coming together to raise money for local charities.

"So that's what it takes to get into *the* social circle. I've heard about that party Annie. Quite the event if you call the NGL a charity!"

"What do you mean?"

"They work that party—with one hand out and the other holding a cocktail."

"You two must come." Jack Morris was on his way to the pressroom. "Everyone wants to meet Catalano/Rossi. They've been following your articles. I'll send my car for you Catalano—and that cousin of yours too. It's an interesting mix of the who's who. Rossi, be at her place by 7." Playing the game had gotten Annie closer to uncovering what was really going on. She felt it. Annie couldn't wait to tell Daniel later that evening. Right now she was on her way to see Emily at the market. She'd already put out a full day's work.

Annie and Emily had become quite close in a short amount of time. In a way, Emily was like looking in the mirror. She kept informed. She'd read all of what Catalano/Rossi had written. She found the articles repulsive. Such headlines worked just the opposite with Emily and the other Amish women. They'd confided in Annie Finley that they would be listening to the President speak. They respected the woman's strength, sensing she spoke from the heart. Emily felt especially close to Isabel Romero—a bond only a mother could understand. Annie understood—but she couldn't say a thing to Emily. Not yet that is.

The Party

TOMMY SPENT THE MORNING PREPARING HORS d'oeuvres. If there was a reason to be in the kitchen Tommy grabbed it. Annie called Carmen, inviting him over a few hours before the limousine's arrival. Some of Tommy's associates were stopping by to meet his cousin from Boston. It certainly would be an interesting Saturday. Annie stayed with Daniel until after lunchtime. He was making great progress. An intense physical therapy program had been mapped out for him. Doctors realized once he returned home, the only physical therapy he'd receive would be in the fields. Spring planting was not far away. Daniel wanted to be ready. Annie told Daniel about the event she'd be going to later that evening. He had only one request.

"I WANT TO SEE YOU DRESSED as one of those women in your magazines. You are more beautiful than any of them. I miss the warmth of you beside me."

"And I miss you. I'll make arrangements to visit later."

Knowing Daniel was with her every step of the way spurred Annie on.

Stopping at the gift shop to make the change back to Annie Catalano, she asked Pauline a favor.

"No problem," Pauline told her. "I'll take care of everything."

Returning to the studio Annie was greeted by tempting aromas coming from the kitchen. "Something smells good Tommy. I'm glad you're going with us tonight."

"It's my pleasure. You've made a name for yourself Annie. You make the Catalanos proud!"

"Thanks cousin. Just playing the game."

"For you to go into that hornet's nest and accomplish what you have in such a short time amazes me. You have a gift for the pen; far superior to others who've been on that staff for years including Jack Morris himself. Wait 'til you see his place. One of those spreads tucked away on Society Hill."

"That doesn't surprise me. Carmen told me there's lots of old money there."

Annie went to get dressed while Tommy finished in the kitchen.

Soon the place was full of artsy types. As everyone nibbled on Tommy's delicacies, conversation flowed—from the upcoming Art Spectacular to be held in unison with the President's visit to those features written by the Catalano/Rossi team. Red wine was flowing and so were opinions. Some were supportive of the Times attacks; others disgusted by their tactics.

"As an artist I support our freedom of speech but that 2nd Amendment is another story. Preying on the children is not the prey intended."

Annie wanted to voice agreement with this woman who Tommy told her was organizing demonstrations in support of President Romero. But she couldn't. Just hearing the NGL demonstrators would face competition out on Constitution Plaza as the President spoke gave Annie faith that what she wrote was not taken as truth by many Jack Morris was out to sway.

"Now now. This is a friendly gathering. No more politics." Tommy interrupted his friend. He realized neither side would be budging.

"You look stunning." Tommy led Annie away from the others.

Dressed in a sleek, sleeveless emerald green taffeta dress with a low V-neckline showcased a confident woman. Accented with clusters of gemstones and black patent shoes, Annie left nothing undone. Her long hair with those perfect highlights added more allure to the total package.

"Tommy is right Annie. You look beautiful."

"This cousin of mine is a fascinating woman Carmen."

"I'm learning that more and more."

Checking the time, Tommy wrapped the impromptu gathering up—and just in time. A knock on the door signaled their ride had arrived.

Sleek, black as night, the limo with tinted windows took Annie's breath away. Not because of its plush interior or fully-stocked bar. Rather it was the images rushing through her mind as the driver held the door open.

"Champagne anyone?"

Carmen didn't hesitate. "I'll have a touch Tommy."

"Annie?"

"No thanks."

It was a spectacular winter night. Stars glittering like diamonds proved to be the perfect backdrop for Society Hill.

Carmen was the ideal tour guide. "This is the largest concentration of original 18th and early 19th century rowhouses in the country; both Federal and Georgian style. My father told me it's where our past meets the future."

It was impossible to take it all in. It didn't matter. Their limo was pulling up to the Morris' brick home tastefully lit in tiny white lights. A man dressed in Federal-style garb opened the door. Brushing away any snow that may have entered, he put his hand out for Annie.

"Madam."

Leading her down the cobblestone walk, he paused in front of the narrow door with its many panes to wait for the two taking their time behind them.

"So this is what all those headlines buy."

"What happens to all of it when the presses stop?" wondered Tommy.

Antiques, original art, and a winding staircase with a crystal chandelier—this Federal estate fit the description of the neighborhood. Anyone who was anything was in attendance. Even before they could get their coats off, Jack Morris was there to greet them

"There's that ace reporter Catalano. This must be Cousin Tommy. Enjoyed reading about your archway. We sold extra papers with that feature. Good for everyone—if you know what I mean. Rossi, glad you could make it."

"It's a pleasure meeting you sir. Thank you for inviting me. That feature turned out to be good for my business as well." Tommy gave Annie a wink as Carmen stayed silent.

Stopping a young woman serving champagne, Morris invited his guests to take a glass. This time Annie joined in.

"Let me introduce you."

There were so many people with so many titles; administrators and educators; politicians; those responsible for preserving Philadelphia's heritage. There were the curious and those with lesser titles or none at all. Of course every member of the Morris family was present—including Steve. Staff photographers were snapping photos of the Who's Who.

It had to happen. The first of the NGL executives was introduced to Catalano/Rossi. After praising the reporters, he turned serious.

"That last feature with that photo was the clincher. I'd run it every day before she gets here. It will be worth your while."

He was followed by more and more NGL top brass—all saying the same thing in their own way; all downing champagne and gorging themselves on escargot.

Looking for a quick escape, Annie asked for a ladies' room. Directed up the stairway, down the hall, 2nd door on the right, she excused herself. But with so much to take in, Annie entered the 2nd door on the left. Without thinking why it was so dark, she reached for a light switch—and found one.

"What to hell's going on? Get to hell out of here! Turn that damn light out!"

Taking a second to get her bearings, Annie quickly realized she was in a bedroom—a most massive room with a most massive bed. Smack in the middle of that bed was Susan Morris; her hair in disarray; lipstick smeared. Although the moment only lasted for a second Annie did note the guy was quite young and handsome. His blonde hair was as messed up as Susan's.

"Oh I am so sorry. I was looking for the ladies' room."

"Across the damn hallway Catalano. Shut the light off and leave!"

After powdering her nose, she headed back down the hallway—quietly so as not to disturb the lovers. Lining the walls were portraits of generations of Morris. She stopped to read a few of the bios.

"My oh my! What a beauty. You play dress-up quite well. Want to play take clothes off like my niece is doing?"

"I'm not into games. Excuse me."

Steve Morris was blocking her way.

"Oh I think you're a player. I'm not sure whose side you're on."

"I don't take sides. I just do my job."

"Good answer. Now tell me this Catalano. It's Catalano isn't it?"

"It's Morris isn't it?"

"Very cute. You forget I have reporter blood flowing through my veins. I can find out what you were doing at that hospital; find out why were dressed up in that morbid outfit. Kinky—for sure! So tell me what you're up to Annie. I like games."

He reached out; pulling her closer. Annie jerked backward, telling him she had no clue what he was talking about.

"Feisty little woman. I like a fighter. I really do. Don't make me have to be a mean little boy."

He walked back down the stairs.

Making sure he kept going, Annie continued past more portraits—all looking at her in the same manner as Steve Morris.

"Reporting isn't the only similarity flowing through their veins," she thought going down those stairs and back into the crowd.

"Where were you Annie? I've been looking for you. There's someone you must meet."

Stopping one of those servers carrying a tray, Annie took a glass of champagne and followed her boss. Violins and piano keys could be heard in the background as he guided her around guests standing and drinking—pretending to be involved in conversation when actually looking to see who was with whom and who they could impress.

"I told you I'd find her."

A man—himself engrossed in what looked to be one of those pretentious conversations turned around when he heard Jack behind him.

"Annie Catalano. Meet Charlie Lawton, CEO of the NGL."

If Jack Morris only knew she'd just met Charlie up in bed with his granddaughter. But Catalano was smooth. It came with the territory.

"I'm glad to finally meet you Mr. Lawton. Mr. Morris has told me so much about you."

"All good I hope."

"Most definitely."

He was young. Much younger than she'd imagined the head of such a powerful, conniving association would be. He went on and on about those features she and Carmen had written.

"Pardon me. Be right back." Jack Morris left them to fend for themselves.

Annie never did have a minute with the man. Susan came from nowhere; clinging to his side as if they were still in bed. Neither mentioned the incident. Just part of doing business Annie figured; his way of paying for all that free press. Catalano was learning that favors come in all sorts of packages.

"What's the President's schedule?" Mr. Lawton was all business now.

"It hasn't been released Charlie. With all the heightened interest I doubt if it will be. Our website's telling everyone to arrive early the day before. Obviously no protestors will be getting anywhere near her but we will be heard. There are other ways to get one's message across. We're counting on Catalano/Rossi."

"We're with you Mr. Lawton."

Annie knew she had to say the right thing or she'd be called back into Susan Morris' office for another tongue thrashing.

"We've posted that photo of Romero and her rifles on our website. It's had thousands of hits. We look forward to this confrontation. News bureaus from around the globe will be covering her attempt to bring change to our core rights. Let them see democracy in action."

"It will be something to witness."

"Are you interviewing the woman?"

"No assignments have been given."

"Susan. I think a woman interviewing another woman would make a great read. Ms. Catalano could tap into that female thing."

"We have our press passes. I'll talk to Grandfather."

"Remember what we were talking about," he whispered in a hushed tone. "This is one of those opportunities where you can take the lead—make the decision. Start setting yourself apart from the rest of your family; when the time comes, this all falls into your lap." He pulled Susan closer.

So who controls the Times Union thought Annie? For a little more putting out Charlie Lawton could eventually call more shots than he probably already was doing.

"I'm back. I wanted to be certain we had extra outlets in place for our papers next week. The city will be overflowing with people. Keepsake editions are major money makers. Susan—make sure every paper is designated as a Keepsake—above the fold. Use the Presidential seal; slap on some flags. This is what we've needed to eat up some of those lost revenues. The newspaper remains a living testament to history. You can hold it. Keep it. Read it over and over. You can't do that with cable or radio."

"You sold me!"

"Charlie. It's not you people that I worry about."

"With a reporter like Catalano you can keep fabricating headlines. Bad news sells."

"Indeed it does. And Catalano has mastered the art."

'Did I hear the word art?"

"Sure did Tommy. We were talking how this cousin of yours is good at her job. Must be in the genes."

"I'll take that as a compliment."

"Well you can take me home. Rossi and I have to work tomorrow. Speaking of Rossi, where is he?"

"Last I saw him he was reading those framed newspapers up the stairway; all down the hallway."

"I'll find him. You can tell everyone about the Art Spectacular you have planned for next week Tommy. Maybe you can get some free publicity!"

Making sure Steve was still occupied, Annie ran back upstairs. Carmen wasn't anywhere to be seen. She wasn't surprised. If there was history to be read, he'd read every last word. She kept walking, quietly calling his name. Reaching the end of the hallway, Annie veered to the right, noting a door halfway open at the farther end. She kept whispering his name; still no answer. Approaching the door, Annie heard what sounded like the clicking of a computer. That clicking abruptly stopped. Annie hastened back down the hall and into a corner room. No one was in there. Keeping the door open a crack, she kept watch. That's when her cell rang. Frantically she fumbled through her bag and turned it off. In that split second someone exited the room, going the other way down a back stairway. Annie caught but a glimpse of a shadow dashing away. She was certain it was a man. Waiting, she tiptoed down to that room. Whoever fled left a desk light on. Annie kept calling for Carmen as she edged her way inside. Reaching the desk, she sat down. Scraps of paper were scattered. Some were in piles. Legal pads had lists and names and times. There were maps with areas circled in bold. Her heart beating; her eyes shifting from the door to the desk, Annie was drawn to one list in particular. Scribbled in pencil were names familiar to her; names of roads, people, towns, and hamlets. She felt unsettled; that same feeling when seeing those cars with tinted windows invading a way of life in which they had no place. Now she was the invader looking about walls hosting prize trophies from hunting adventures. Jack Morris' study was everything Susan had described.

A sense of urgency propelled Annie to grab a sheet of paper. Her palms sweating, Annie copied down names and targeted areas. Stuffing the paper inside her purse, Annie left the room to those looking at her in a dead stare. She thought about hiding in the corner room to see who might show up but she didn't want to risk being found out. It'd be her luck Steve Morris would be the one showing up.

It didn't take her long to find Carmen. He seemed to be working his way to the backstairs.

"What are you doing here Annie?"

"I came looking for you and found myself in Jack's study. You should have seen all those mounted heads!"

"No thanks."

"You're not a hunter Carmen?"

"No. I couldn't shoot a flea. But anyone who wants to should have that right."

"Let's not get into it tonight. We'll be writing about it all next week."

"I meant to tell you. My parents would like you to join us for dinner Monday. I talk so much about you that they'd like to meet my writing partner. Tommy's invited too."

"I'd love to meet them Carmen. Just give us a time and place and we'll be there." Reaching the bottom step, Annie was stopped by a Morris she'd had no real interaction with up to this point.

"Ms. Catalano. Do you have a minute?"

"I'll find Tommy."

Carmen excused himself while Annie stayed back to talk with Susan's cousin Joe, the paper's ad director.

"I've been meaning to stop and tell you how your articles have affected ad sales—in a positive way. Our lineage has moderately increased. I hate to think what will happen once the President has come and gone."

"What do you mean?"

"Right now there's the anticipation of the confrontation. Readers are buying the paper to see what you have to say. It's a build-up to the event. But I fear once the crowds have dispersed our presses will stop. It's that serious. In fact, it's even more serious than my grandfather realizes. He's a newsman through and through. He thinks he has a handle on it all but he doesn't. He's wearing blinders as advertisers are dropping like flies."

"Why?"

"Why are they dropping away?"

"Yes. Why are you losing them?"

"No simple answer; a new type of competition and a stubborn old man who won't change how we publish."

"It sounds like he might have to change."

"A true Morris publishes headlines that insinuate. You know that Ms. Catalano. You do it every day. Twisting the truth; that's our style of journalism. It worked in the past but communication has drastically changed. Advertisers have so many options as do consumers seeking the news."

"Why not meet with your grandfather?"

"He's not rational when I present the truth in black and white. Even more irrational is Susan. Her claws are out. She's a cold, heartless woman who wants to head Morris Publishing and she'll do anything to get there. She tells me to push the sales team harder. That's why advertising has such a turnover. The stress is too much. On a personal note, it cost me my marriage. The way stocks are going it might cost me even more."

"I wish I had an answer Joe. I know nothing of how your department works. I have hard enough time writing in the style your family demands."

"Forgive me for unloading on you. Guess we all better brace ourselves for the week ahead."

"You can unload anytime Joe. Try to keep it in perspective. There are always reasons to be thankful. You are never alone."

"I thank you for listening. Good night Ms. Catalano."

"Please call me Annie. Good night Joe."

Guests were starting to leave as Annie found Carmen talking with their boss. Moments later Tommy showed up with their coats. After pleasantries were exchanged, they headed to the vestibule in wait of their limo. That's when Charlie stopped them; repeating his encouragement to keep up the heat. Susan slurred a good-night. Champagne had taken its toll. As the front door opened Annie happened to look back over her shoulder in time to catch a glimpse of a young man—the spitting image of Ira's son Jonas. It couldn't be Annie rationalized as the door shut. Could it?

After the limo dropped Carmen at his apartment overlooking Rittenhouse Square, the driver headed to Tommy's. That's when Annie informed Tommy she was going on to see Daniel.

"But Annie, it's late. You'll never get up to see him."

"It's all arranged."

"Be careful. I told Heather I'd watch over you," Tommy stated getting out of the limo. Annie told Tommy not to worry. "Jacob too is watching over me."

A Moment Alone

THE CITY WAS STRIKINGLY BEAUTIFUL AT night; more so than in the harshness of day. With fewer people in a hurry, the buildings and parks and little curiosities held a character invisible in the rush of 9–5. As the limo drove into the hospital circle Annie remembered she'd had a call. It was Pauline, saying some Bishop with a long beard had stopped by to see Daniel. Because Daniel had been asleep, he told the nurse he'd be back in the morning.

Why would the Bishop come to Philadelphia, Annie thought? Now she'd really have to be discreet. Between Steve Morris and the Bishop, Annie could not make a mistake.

It went just as Pauline said it would. No one stopped her. No one at the nurse's station even looked up. Annie went into Daniel's room and shut the door without talking to a single person. A light had been left on in the bathroom; that door left ajar. If Annie looked over rooftops through the large window panes near Daniel's bed, it was as if she was looking out their bedroom window. All she could see were those white stars and that bright full moon.

He was sound asleep. Annie took his hand in hers and kissed it. Sitting at the edge, she stroked his hair back off his forehead; her finger following the shape of his face down to his chin. Tears rolled down her cheeks with thoughts of Jacob. Would he have married? Would he have had children? Would he have stayed to farm the land; keep watch over pastures and fields which generations before had tended? Maybe he would have pursued his love of music. How she missed her little boy and this man now stirring and opening his eyes. Wiping away her tears, Daniel sat up and drew her near. Brushing her hair off her shoulders; pulling her coat away, he kissed the nap of her neck; then brought her lips to his—kissing her gently.

"Don't talk my love," whispered Annie seconds later. "You wanted to see me dressed like one of those women in my magazines."

Standing, Annie let her coat fall to the floor; then her dress.

"I want to lie with you Daniel. I need you to hold me."

With the wind singing their song, they laid together once more. They talked for what seemed hours. That was nothing new. They did the same back home. Annie told Daniel what she'd found scribbled on top of Morris' desk. She told him how she thought she saw Jonas at the party.

"What do you think it all means Daniel?"

"First of all if that was Jonas, why would he be here? Is it for women or drugs or just the thrill of getting out of our community? He didn't have to come to Philadelphia when he could have gone anywhere. Why Philadelphia and why that house and why now? There has to be a connection Annie; has to be a reason for his being here; a reason so many of our roads and highways are on a list in the very home he is in."

"The maps took in a massive area of the county Daniel; going right down Co. Rt. 68. Something rotten is going on and I fear our Jacob died because of it."

Holding each other a little tighter, their silence spoke volumes. Grieving had to wait; for now their sorrow would be expressed by their actions. So they continued discussing the 2nd Amendment; her friendship with Emily; her guilt in writing those misleading articles. He told her she looked beautiful in her fancy dress. And sometime between 3 and 4 a.m. they fell asleep.

A CART BEING WHEELED PAST HIS room awoke Daniel as the sun was peeking over the horizon. He knew the nurse would be in with his meds.

The staff had left them alone for as long as they could. Another familiar sound caused Daniel concern. It was the Bishop; his harsh voice echoing down the hallway asking for Daniel Finley, explaining this was the only time he had to visit. Daniel feared he'd barge right in.

Daniel woke Annie. "Quick Annie. The Bishop is right outside. Grab your clothes; go in the bathroom and lock the door. It leads into the next room. He'll never see you leave."

Jumping out of the bed, Annie scooped up her clothes, kissed Daniel good-bye and was shutting the door just as the Bishop stepped into the room.

"You must have been talking in your sleep Daniel." Annie listened to the old man as she quietly got dressed. But she didn't wait around to hear all of what he had to say. Buttoning her coat, she tiptoed past a patient on oxygen in the adjoining room; then made her way out of the hospital. By the time she made it back to the studio, Tommy had the coffee perking.

The Assignment

MONDAY MORNING WAS SHEER CHAOS IN Philadelphia. The President, accompanied by Vice-President Parker, would be arriving late Wednesday. The White House announced she would be speaking Thursday at noon in front of Independence Hall. Streets in the Historic Park area were blocked off. Traffic was a nightmare. Snipers were making last minute surveillance checks.

"Those aren't the only tunnels," shouted Carmen, watching a television commentator on a flat screen hanging up in front of him. TVs surrounded the newsroom. This one particular reporter was talking about Philly's subway and commuter rail systems, including pedestrian tunnels near connecting stations.

"What do you mean Carmen?"

"I was referring to the forgotten tunnels."

"Forgotten?"

"There are tunnels in this city never used; built in anticipation of expansion that never happened. You'd be surprised where some are located. Anyway, don't forget—dinner tonight. 7 p.m. at Louie's. I have a feeling if I don't mention it now I never will. Morris is already hollering."

Over the intercom came the summons to the conference room.

"Here we go Annie. Let's see what lies he wants us to write now."

"You okay?"

"Family thing—you know how that goes."

"Sure do."

"It's my father. I never seem to be able to meet his expectations."

"I get that feeling with my mother."

"Is your mother a writer?"

"Why do you ask?"

"Curious. They say the apple doesn't fall far from the tree. I'll admit I've inherited my father's respect of and hunger for history."

"My mother has babies."

"Think you ever will Annie?"

"I think we better get prepared."

That meant notepads and plenty of pencils.

Walking through the door, Carmen complimented Annie on having her photo in the Sunday paper with Charlie Lawton.

"I don't remember the photo being taken. I'm surprised it ran so soon."

"If Jackie Boy wants it in they'll stop the presses to make it happen."

"Come on. Let's go. Bring in more chairs if you have to." The Jack Morris of Saturday night had changed back into the screaming publisher. Even before everyone was seated he started in. About twenty minutes later, Susan came rushing through the door.

"Sorry I'm late. I've been on the phone with the White House. Catalano you're interviewing the President Wednesday at 7p.m. This will be her only interview. They're announcing this morning that over the next thirteen weeks President Romero will be visiting the thirteen states that represent the thirteen original colonies. They're calling it her, "Path to Democracy" Tour. The goal is to walk in the footsteps of those who formed our union while at the same time building the case for change— subtly pointing out the interpretation of words written then and their meaning today."

"The fundamentals must not change. It's that basic. Great job Susan! Great job! Who cares what they call it. Means we can scoop the competition on Thursday even before she speaks. Catalano you have to get in there and make her slip. Then write the feature of your career. Go for the Pulitzer, I don't care; just get the angle. Your byline interview will make papers fly off the shelves. I want front page layouts this morning. Give it some sidebars—flags. I want that photo of her with her rifles in every day this week. Every single day do you hear me?"

No one spoke. That meant they heard him.

"We need a map showing people where they can park; where they can assemble. Show them the streets closed off and points where they can gain access to hear her speak. Crowds are expected to be enormous—as are the protestors. I want photos; interview the people. Catch the feel of the masses. Susan—go over our distribution plans again and again. No outlet is too small. If we don't have the papers on the streets we can't sell them. Get more honor boxes out there. Steve—You'll be on desk Wednesday night. You and Catalano will give final approval to that front page once it's written and on the page. It's the biggest press run since 9/11. I'd stay but I have to be at a benefit in her honor—rather ironic I admit."

"I'm sure Catalano and I will work just fine together," spoke Steve. "She certainly has a kick to her writing style. I like that."

Annie didn't look across the room. Her mind was filled with the fact that she, a young Amish woman from the back roads of northern New York, would be interviewing the President of the United States. Her time to write the truth was now.

Jack Morris pushed a button on the intercom. "Get me Joe on the phone."

Moments later over speaker phone, he lit into the head of advertising.

"What do you mean ad sales haven't increased for this week? You have the President coming to town and you can't sell ads? Listen to me. Get your team out of the office and sell the damn space. I want you selling too. There is no excuse for poor lineage this week. Sell it or get to hell out!"

Slamming down the receiver, he turned his wrath to those around him.

"This could be our comeback. Let me rephrase that. This will be our comeback to #1. That's where we've always been and I will take down anyone who stands in our way. Print has been the voice for democracy since this country began and no one or no other medium will bring us down. Now get out of my face and go to work."

Carmen stood. "Mr. Morris. Since Catalano will be preparing for the interview, what is it you'd like me to work on? If it's more history, I think I have that department covered."

"You are the weaker link in Catalano/Rossi. You can't always count on others to carry you so I suggest you go find your material. Get your head out of the history books for a change. They're all dead. Live in the moment. Go talk to real people."

A knock at the door cut the tension.

"Excuse me. A young woman is here to see Ms. Catalano. She said it was urgent. I heard you dismiss everyone Mr. Morris."

"I did. And they are leaving—Now!"

Waiting while others rushed to the door, Annie glanced out across the newsroom to the reception area. At first she was disbelieving of the image she saw standing there. Surprise turned to fear. What was Emily doing in downtown Philly on a Monday morning at the Times Union asking for Annie Catalano? Feeling trapped, Annie lingered. She'd never mentioned the paper to Emily; never said her last name was Catalano. Annie's heart was pounding.

"Oh look Catalano. One of your kin has come a visiting! Maybe she brought you some fresh-baked bread. If she has time I'd love to meet her—if you know what I mean."

"I've never met her. I have no clue why that woman is here to see me."

"Little defensive are we. That's a sure sign you're hiding something. I will find out your story. You best go tend to your guest. She must have cows to milk. I'm looking forward to sharing duties with you Wednesday night."

Annie ignored his comments. It did worry her that he suspected something and it would be just like him to dig for the dirt, then hold it over her but right now she had to deal with Emily staring at her. Stopping to grab her coat, it was obvious Carmen wanted to talk.

"Someone's waiting for me. We can talk later."

"I'll be out on the street. You heard Morris."

"And you know how irrational he can be."

It didn't take Annie long to figure out why Emily had come. She was holding yesterday's paper.

"We have to talk Annie Catalano."

"Not here," replied Annie, leading Emily to the elevator.

They said nothing; not until they were in the lobby and Annie was putting on her coat.

"Let's go for a walk."

Two blocks away from the paper, Annie was the first to speak.

"You saw the photo with me in it and you're wondering why I mislead you. Right?"

"You did not mislead me Ms. Catalano. You lied. Everything you've told me has been a lie. You led me to believe you cared. I confided in you. I trusted you. You not only used me and my son but my entire community. Every one of those women thought you understood; felt there was something different about you with which they connected. You're a liar. You lied on the soul of my dead child. This photo is blaspheme. You stand with the devil Ms. Catalano. God will judge your actions."

Emily began to walk away.

"Wait! Wait Emily."

"Do not use my name."

Taking hold of Emily's arm, Annie stopped her from crossing the street.

"You preach forgiveness. You preach living in God's presence." Turning Emily around, Annie continued, taking hold of both her arms and speaking calmly but firmly; making Emily look her in the eye.

"I ask you to trust me Emily. I am walking in a path that God has laid out for me. I can say nothing more. Believe me when I tell you that what we shared I hold dear and what I said was the truth. Open your heart and listen. You do believe. I heard it in words spoken. I see it in the sadness of your eyes. At the end of this journey I will seek your friendship again. I ask for your understanding and your prayers."

Letting go, Annie hesitated at the curb; then darted through traffic, heading back to the office.

"So how goes the homestead? Did you tell her I'm available?" Steve Morris was on his way out of the newsroom. Annie ignored him. She had an interview to prepare for and dinner at 7 p.m.—sharp.

Dinner Conversation

RUSH HOUR TRAFFIC WAS SNARLED IN every direction. With main routes closed and bridges over the Delaware backed up, commuters were forced to move at a snail's pace. It didn't matter the mode of transportation, the entire city was at a dead crawl.

Annie flagged a cab; thinking the driver might know some secret route. But he didn't. They crept with the rest of the cabbies and SUVs and buses—all trying to out maneuver the other. The situation did afford Annie a close up look of the crowds already gathered. Many seemed to be bedded down in tents until the President's appearance. The NGL had been successful in recruiting loyal supporters. Anti-Romero signs were everywhere. Men, women and children—many dressed in camouflage and toting the American flag or wearing it seemed poised for confrontation.

The 2nd Amendment certainly brought out the people Annie thought, deciding to call Pauline in hopes of getting a message to Daniel. She was in luck. Pauline answered. She was still at work and had a message for Annie.

"Your husband wants me to tell you he misses you and to stay safe."

"Please tell Daniel I miss him too. And let him know I will be interviewing the President on Wednesday. I won't see him until after her visit but tell him not to worry. We will be going home the end of this week."

"The President! Great work Annie. I'll be waiting to read your article. I have to tell you I don't believe a word you write. I know better—if you know what I mean. Are you going to get into the issue with the President?"

"You could say that Pauline."

Somehow the driver made exceptional time getting to Tommy's. Probably had something to do with the extra tip she'd promised. Annie learned how things worked in the city.

Taking a quick shower, she was ready by 6:30. It was Tommy who was lingering; still preparing for the Art Spectacular scheduled to open Wednesday.

"Heather called earlier to tell you that Artist Gregory will be accompanying the President. Many of his friends will be in town to show their support. Even Heather and Alicen will be coming tomorrow afternoon. It's going to be something."

"Before I forget I have some news. Susan Morris set up an interview with the President."

"She should have set it up with you. I've read some of her stuff. She doesn't have what it takes even though it's in her DNA."

"She did."

"She did what?"

"I'm doing the interview."

Tommy was pleased. "I guess she knows how to sell papers."

Minutes later they were in a cab heading to Louie's. Annie found herself wondering about Carmen and his parents. She was certain she'd hear a bit of history during dinner.

For a Monday night in February the traffic was more like Times Square on New Year's Eve. But then, it wasn't just another Monday night in Philadelphia.

"Good thing Carmen made reservations. Louie's is always busy but this week it will be near impossible to get in without them."

It was impossible to get near the place. The driver dropped them at the corner.

Tommy led the way past those hoping to get in. A gentleman at the door asked if they had reservations. Soon they were being led through the restaurant overlooking the river by a young waitress dressed in black but in a sensual sort of way. The decor was authentic Italy—right down to fountains with Goddesses and wrought iron lattices laden with grapevines.

"If you weren't hungry before you came that aroma of pesto and San Marzano tomatoes cooked in extra virgin olive oil will do the trick."

"How do you know what tomatoes they're using?"

"They have a scent all their own."

"Well it worked. I'm famished."

Stopping in front of a table with pillars covered in ivy as a backdrop, the waitress motioned for them to have a seat. Carmen and his parents were there but they didn't notice their guests standing in front of them. They were too busy quizzing each other.

"You got that one right. How about the 9th one?"

"New Hampshire."

"Right again. The 1st?"

"Virginia?"

"What! How could you forget the first? The first one Carmen?"

The waitress was back, standing in front of the table.

"Excuse me," she politely spoke. "Your guests are here."

"Oh. I'm sorry." Carmen seemed embarrassed. "We get into our own world with our back and forth. Please. Please sit down."

Tommy pulled out a chair for Annie. Introductions were made. His parents were just as Annie expected; stoic yet polite in an academic sort of way. The father was dressed in tweeds. His mustache and bow tie fit the title of Dean of History. Mrs. Rossi was slim—a bit round shouldered with glasses and hair pulled back into a French twist. Her tightly drawn lips flat lined her demeanor as did the muted suit and genuine pearls.

"If you don't mind my asking, what was the number one that you were referring to Mr. Rossi?"

"I see why you beat our Carmen for the interview Ms. Catalano. In answer to your question and as Carmen explained, we go back and forth all the time. Mrs. Rossi and I ask the questions and Carmen provides the answers."

"Most times he does," added Mrs. Rossi. "He is a student of history as we are."

"I've become aware of his knowledge. He told me that's why he chose to live in Philadelphia."

"Carmen is here to make history."

"He told me that too."

"A Rossi lives by principles and defends such axioms to the end. To live in a land of great opportunity demands loyalty. Our Carmen realizes his responsibility and through the written word he will make his mark."

"Don't make me blush Father. *I have no other view than to promote the public good, and am unambitious of honors not founded in the approbation of my Country.*

"A fitting quote Carmen. Our first President spoke eloquently no matter what the circumstances; setting the tone for the forty some that have followed." Mr. Rossi then turned his attention to Annie. "What is your background Ms. Catalano? What makes you qualified to interview a President?"

"Please, enough of that for now. The waitress is waiting for our order."

Mrs. Rossi's interruption put Annie temporarily at ease. She'd be ready for this father angry that his son had been overshadowed by the newcomer.

"To answer your original question Ms. Catalano," continued Mr. Rossi, "We were quizzing Carmen on the thirteen colonies since this new President has chosen to mock them. I'm shocked you didn't remember the first colony to ratify the Constitution Carmen. It was Delaware. Delaware, Carmen. I've told you that before. Delaware was the first!"

"I don't know how I could have forgotten that Father."

"One more question before we order."

"I'm sure our guests are not amused by our pursuit of the trivia."

"I find it fascinating Mrs. Rossi."

"Thank you Ms. Catalano. So one more it is. Which colony recommended the Bill of Rights?"

Carmen's silence was deafening. It was Tommy who spoke.

"If you don't mind Carmen, I'd like to try my luck."

"So the artist wants to play?"

"I'll give it a shot Mr. Rossi. I've been doing some research in honor of the President's visit. It's all part of a promotion for our Art Spectacular."

"In honor of her mockery?"

"I don't look at it that way. She was elected overwhelmingly by the People. That to me is democracy speaking."

The senior Rossi ignored Tommy's analogy. "What's the answer then?"

"It was Virginia. And Virginia was the tenth state to ratify the Constitution." Tommy picked up a menu and asked for a glass of wine.

Through appetizers to entrees the conversation was polite yet guarded. The only light moment came served with dessert.

"Great tiramisu," exclaimed Tommy. "I find the trick is to dip—not soak—the lady fingers in the strong espresso."

"I'd prefer to soak it in the liquor," responded Mr. Rossi.

They all shared a smile and continued to do so as the waitress poured the limoncello into small-stemmed after dinner glasses.

"Not a drinker of liqueurs Ms. Catalano? Try it. The lemons add just enough tartness to the flavor."

"It is delightful Mr. Rossi." Annie tried a few sips wondering why anyone would spoil such a marvelous meal with such a disgusting drink.

When the bill was presented with mints to the side, Mr. Rossi insisted on paying.

Parting ways at the front door, Tommy flagged a cab. Even though it was after nine, crowds had only increased.

"I feel bad for Rossi," spoke Tommy. "I could tell he had no clue what his father was asking."

"I can't imagine living under that father's microscope. Too bad Carmen's an only child. The pressure is on him to perform."

Annie thought for a brief second that there were advantages to having an abundance of siblings. Of course she was thinking in terms of less than fourteen.

Getting Ready

TUESDAY WAS A DAY OF PREPARATION. Before arriving early at the paper she checked in with Pauline. Thanks to physical therapy and determination, Daniel was stronger than ever; ready to go home.

Annie made it to the paper earlier than usual with the intent on staying as late as necessary. Her plan was to research the President's platform; go through her campaign speeches and promises and get a little more of her personal background that hadn't been finagled in headlines. Carmen was quiet, pumping out a "story for the history books" he explained when coming up for air. All the Morris' were present, making it obvious that this was *the* moment for the Times Union. From television sets came images of those thousands gathered; some were protesting; some were in support of Romero. Others were curious bystanders.

A steady stream of politicians and those heading interest groups went in and out of Jack Morris' office. Susan stood by her grandfather's side. Once between meetings Annie heard Jack screaming at his grandson Joe. "If I have to get out and do your job for you I will. I've sold advertising. I know how it's done and damn you if you can't do it given the circumstances you'll never be able to do it. I want a report by 3 as to where you and your staff stand with revenues generated for this week alone. If I don't see results you just might see the door hitting you on the way out." Annie looked up in time to see Susan patting her grandfather on the back.

Around eleven Annie was called into the conference room. Waiting for her was Charlie Lawton with Susan sitting between him and her grandfather.

"I can see you are preparing for tomorrow. Just wanted to go over what you need to do."

It was Lawton giving the pep talk. "You've proven you can do it Ms. Catalano. Don't let the Office intimidate you. Look her in the eyes. She's just another person you will be interviewing. Treat her the same way as any of the others you've interviewed. Don't be distracted by the Secret Service. Don't let her take command of the conversation. She has a tendency to do so. It's her way of avoiding questions; changing the subject."

"Take your time writing the piece. It won't have to go to press before 4 a.m. That will give you up to the last minute to make any changes. Go over every word. One word can change the entire piece. Once you and Steve have signed off on it, send it to the press room. Call and tell them when the final version is on its way. We can't afford any mistakes." It was apparent Susan was anxious for that paper to hit the streets. She'd covered all the angles.

"All the racks and honor boxes will have this promo sheet on display." Jack showed Annie the brightly colored stock with bold print. There was no doubt in anyone's mind that it would be seen. So would Annie's byline. "I've been working on those front page layouts. I like this one. Of course once we get that story of yours, this will have to be altered somewhat."

"Strong layout Jack; great use of space. Love the flag at the top; that Commemorative header. Any reference to patriotism always stirs the folks. It's like a call to arms," laughed Charlie.

"Times Roman makes the difference. Bold and black certainly makes the statement. It always has. That will sell the damn thing no matter if it's a Republican, Democrat, gun lover or gun hater buying it! It worked when both Kennedys and King were assassinated. It worked when Lincoln fell to a bullet."

"We'll push papers under the guise of a 'Commemorative Edition' all week long. Radio certainly can't capitalize on this like we can; neither can that damn internet."

"What are the assignments during her speech?"

"I'm working on that this afternoon Susan," replied Jack.

"How about some lunch? I'm buying!"

"We know who'll be buying if you pay for it Charlie!"

"You're on to me Susan," laughed Charlie. "I'm starving. Let's eat. Jack and Annie—care to join us?"

"I wouldn't venture out into that crowd if I had to—and I don't have to yet. You two go along. Catalano and I have work to do." The stubborn old editor went back into his office. Annie went back to her screen.

"Hey Catalano," yelled Charlie across the news room. "Go after that President. You have what it takes."

"Thanks Mr. Lawton." Annie didn't have to be told that. All she had to do was think of her little one.

After an hour or so of staring at her computer she leaned over and asked Carmen if he wanted to order something to eat.

"No. I'm still full from last night. You go ahead."

"That was great food Carmen. I never thought I'd be hungry again but I am. Your parents are definite scholars. I can see where you get your thirst for knowledge."

"I'll never meet their standards. I knew Delaware was the first. I knew about Virginia."

"As long as you meet your own standards, that's what matters. Others expectations are out of our control."

"I think this story should do it Annie. They won't be able to miss this. Morris won't be burying this one on some inside page. It's one for the history books. Remember that Catalano."

"Give me a clue."

"Give me a break. You're the one with the big interview. You heard the old man. I'm the weaker link of Catalano—Rossi."

"Again. Just another's opinion."

That was the end of their conversation. Annie made outlines of questions while Carmen kept slamming the keyboard. Around 5:30 he turned his computer off and left without saying a word. Annie stayed until around 8. With a plan intact, she went back to Tommy's. She knew Heather and Alicen were in town. Her plan was to see them before the interview the next day.

Meeting the President

ANNIE COULDN'T STOP THINKING ABOUT THE day Mary and Ira were married. It wasn't the ceremony or gifts or her disgust of the union. It was that split second when sitting outback—alone and surrounded by chickens—when she found herself thinking about this woman with whom she'd be meeting in less than two hours. If anyone would have told her how her life would change that coming evening she would have told them to go spend the day in prayer. In three short months she'd gone from farmland to cobblestone; from tending to the two men who were her world to writing about it.

Dressed in a Calvin Klein tailored suit; hair pulled back, make-up flawless and nails manicured, this Amish woman in disguise stepped out of Tommy's studio into a limo provided by her boss. With a black designer bag over her shoulder and leather brief case in hand, Annie represented the look women in business strive to perfect. She'd allowed plenty of time to pass through security. The interview would take place at Independence Hall.

If she were an artist, she decided this city would be her studio. Besides the backdrop, it was awe-inspiring to be in the place where it all began. Jacob would have loved the big bell; the museums. He would have asked so many questions. Annie found solace in the realization that she'd instilled in him a wonder of the world beyond their invisible boundaries. Annie's exuberance for life was evident in Jacob's way of greeting each new day. Sadly his days were too few.

"The President is running a little late Ms. Catalano. She shouldn't be long."

A well-dressed man with credentials around his neck went back out of the room. Annie too had fallen behind schedule, not realizing the multitudes swarming every inch of Philly grew over night. Protestors mobbed the edge of the Park; most marching with flags and signs and images of the President carrying a gun. Annie felt responsible for some of those disgusting placards. Freedom of speech was certainly on display. Once inside the Park, the atmosphere changed to one of Hope and Anticipation. People were milling about; taking pictures or texting. Jumbotrons had been placed throughout the area. Strangers were talking to strangers as if they were best friends. Although the President was not speaking until tomorrow, people on both sides of the Park were ready.

On her way in, a tour guide of Independence Hall had told her she'd be meeting the President in the Assembly Room where both the Constitution and Declaration of Independence had been drafted and signed. Annie felt as if those who'd signed those documents would be walking through the door since desks and pens and other artifacts remained in place. Instead, it was eventually the President of the United States who entered, followed by a stream of Secret Service all wearing sunglasses and ear buds all in a rush.

"I'm sorry to keep you waiting Ms. Catalano. I'm Isabel Romero. I'm very glad to meet you. Let's take a seat."

"I'm glad to meet you Madame President. I thank you for granting me your single interview while in Philadelphia."

"There was a reason you were chosen. Can you guess why?"

"I would think it is because of the articles I've written about you."

"I've read each one of them several times. Although I understand how the press works I know what is fact and what is political spin. I know the Times-Union has never supported anyone expressing any hint of discussion of the 2nd Amendment. Of course when you are heavily supported by the NGL I would expect such allegiance. But none of that is why you were chosen."

Sitting in front of the most powerful person in the world, Annie didn't know what to say or where to take the interview. This tall, striking woman with defined cheekbones and ebony hair pulled tightly back had taken her by surprise. No wonder she trounced her opponent Annie thought as a young woman entered the room carrying a silver tray.

"Tea Ms. Catalano?"

Rattling off flavors, she waited for a reply.

Annie chose the chamomile—with a touch of honey.

"I don't know why there are so many kinds from which to choose. It's like coffee. I'm one who likes a plain cup of coffee. Life is complicated enough without having so many choices."

"Life is certainly complicated Madame President."

They sipped on their brews while making small talk—everything from the setting they found themselves in to the thousands outside voicing their opinions.

"I knew when I made the 2nd Amendment a part of my platform emotions on both sides of the issue would be strong. Add in the political implications and power of special interest groups and we have a fight on our hands. But I am determined. It's time to bring the issue to the forefront."

Annie knew as Annie Catalano this was her time to strike. This was that got-you moment Jack Morris told her to seize. "Take it and run with it," he'd scream. Crass, bold headlines would describe this President as opportunist; anti-American; out to strip loyal citizens of their right to bear arms as etched into the Bill of Rights; using her Office for personal revenge.

But it wasn't Annie Catalano listening to this well-educated woman who knew her stuff.

"I chose to begin this tour in Philadelphia not just because it's the birthplace of our democracy. I chose Philadelphia because, like the entire state of Pennsylvania, it is a haven for gun owners. Their constitutional provision states 'the right of the citizens to bear arms in defense of themselves and the state shall not be questioned.' In addition, no licenses are required to possess rifles and shotguns or to possess handguns in one's home. The 2nd Amendment was not designed to arm and give fire power to just anyone, let alone organized crime here and abroad. It certainly was not designed for random shootings of innocent citizens. I have no problem with guns sold to licensed, screened individuals for hunting or self-protection. But we are becoming a major supplier of sophisticated guns to Mexico. Under federal law, gun dealers are not required to report multiple gun purchases of assault weapons. This is wrong for in the crosshairs of each and every gun, legal and illegal, are innocent victims."

Annie still hadn't scribbled one word.

"This leads me to why I chose to speak with you when all the major networks were scrambling for a few words. I read between the lines of what you'd written. I sensed a pain driving your articles. I knew there was more going on than just a young woman trying to climb the ladder in a right-wing newspaper desperately trying to stay alive. My husband tells me I'm like a detective. I take that as a compliment, especially when confronting complicated issues. I asked that a background check be made of Annie Catalano."

A silence came over the room where great men had argued. President Romero moved closer.

"What I found did not surprise me. A mother's grief is a force that can move mountains. It's the reason our paths have crossed. I sent my beautiful child off to school and four hours later I was identifying her in the morgue; her head blown apart by an illegal assault weapon. I know you are searching for answers. I realize there was no final determination in that horrible accident that took your son's life. I am here to tell you we discovered why and how it ties in to everything I've told you."

Annie tried to stay focused as the reporter but she couldn't. The President was right. She was in Philadelphia for one reason; to get to the bottom of the loss of her child.

"As I have said, our lack of reasonable gun control has led to a black market with guns of every description being smuggled out of this country. We are a supplier of guns that could kill or mame so many more children. Illegal trafficking is a profitable and dangerous business and unfortunately, it is that network that is responsible for Jacob's death."

"So the vehicle that caused the accident was carrying illegal guns?"

"No. That was one of the foot soldiers. It is a piece of the puzzle. We know the Morris Group owned the car. We know they've been involved with illegal activity before. We know their name has been leaked as the main link from Canada to Mexico and their cars, for some reason, are infesting your region of New York but that's all we know. How they get from there to Mexico baffles us."

"Will I be arrested?"

"Arrested! For what—trying to learn the truth? I commend you for that."

The young man at the door walked over to her side, pointing to his watch.

"I have a meeting at City Hall," she explained. "I'm certain you are wondering what the President of the United States is doing getting involved with this investigation. I take personally the death of all citizens young and old who fall victim to a gun crime. When I lost my own child I vowed this had to stop. We can't stop if we don't join together. I was a mother long before I was elected President. I've appointed a task force in the White House that keeps tabs on these incidents. When the Morris vehicle was identified last November in the accident that took your child, the red flag went up to my staff as it occurred on one of their main smuggling routes. In a subtle way your son died as a result of illegal guns. But he did not die in vain. We will get to the bottom of this. I commend you for your strength. One more thing; someone would like to say hello to you—Annie Finley."

Motioning to that young man, he opened the door. In came Artist Gregory. Walking towards him, President Romero told him she'd see him in the morning. Again she thanked Annie and told her she would be in touch. Out she went followed by the Secret Service. A few stayed back in the Assembly Room.

There was so much to talk about but neither Annie nor Artist Gregory had the time. Annie's head was swirling. Somehow she had to put her Catalano hat back on and write. Gregory was on his way to meet his wife. He'd be in town through Friday.

After a few more minutes they said good-bye. Running behind schedule, Annie scraped plans to stop at the hospital. After checking in with Pauline, she instructed the limo driver to take her directly to the paper. Her goal wasn't set on a Pulitzer. It was set on making a difference.

Front Page Story

By the time she was finally sitting at her computer it was after 8. The newsroom was mass confusion with TVs blaring and the AP constantly updating the situation outside. Kicking off heels she couldn't stand and shedding a suit jacket that inhibited her, Annie put her hands to the keyboard.

"Glad you could make it Catalano. I was beginning to think the President won you over."

Steve Morris started right in.

"Actually I did find President Romero quite interesting even though we share different views. If you'll excuse me I have a front page to fill."

"I'll be out of the office for a few hours. Give you some breathing room."

Annie didn't look up; pretending to be into her feature. When out of the corner of her eye she saw the elevator door close, Annie went to work. Once she got to the place where thoughts flowed as freely as the creek in spring, there was no stopping her. It was all coming together; all pouring out in adjectives and verbs and twisting of truths. Jack would be proud of her words chosen and innuendos buried within sentences. Intent on writing an article that would mark the moment at hand, Annie was oblivious to the newsroom clearing out and the clock approaching 1:30 a.m.

"Ms. Catalano. You have a call."

An intern to Susan Morris brought Annie out of the fog.

"Line 2 Ms."

"Thank You." Annie picked up the phone.

"Hey hot stuff. Stevie here. I'm across the street arguing with my favorite bartender. Give you a hint—she's wearing net nylons. I'll be up in a few minutes. Get it Catalano? I'll be *up*!"

Disgusting, thought Annie now fine tuning what she'd written.

"Ms. Catalano. Another call. Line 3."

This time it was Jack Morris, still at his reception for the President who'd made an appearance and long since left for her hotel. Many in attendance stayed to bask in their importance.

"Yes. I'll have Steve call you as soon as he arrives. He must have his cell off. Yes. The interview went very well. You'll be surprised just how well. Thank you, sir, for the opportunity. I'll email you what I have written and wait for your input. Sorry you didn't get to meet her."

A short time later Jack Morris called back. With only minor changes to the story, the hardcore newsman praised Annie for getting the facts straight—his way. "She'll learn we write the news the way *we* see it! This will stop her dead in her tracks. Great job Catalano. I'll send it on to Lawton. Let's get that paper to bed! Have Steve call me as soon as he gets back."

Putting the word bed in the same frame as his grandson was in poor taste Annie thought when hearing the elevator door open. Into the newsroom he came, grinning from ear to ear.

"So did you write the piece of your career?"

"Your grandfather seems to think I did."

"When did he call?"

"Few minutes ago."

"What did you tell him?"

"About what?"

"About where I was."

"I told him I'd have you call when you got back. He tried your cell."

"Would have been back sooner but I've been fishing. Get it? Fishin'?

Net stockings? I'll call the old guy then you and I can get to work before the pressroom panics."

While he was on the phone Annie looked over her material again. That's when her cell phone rang. It was Artist Gregory.

"I realize you're on deadline Annie but I had to call. You've met the President. You've seen first-hand what a decent woman she is."

Annie didn't say anything. She sensed he had to unload.

"I know we live in a democracy but there are some so entrenched in their ideology that they'd do anything to defend it—even if it meant harming the President."

"I believe when you have freedom of speech all voices have that right. Sadly that includes those who've gone over the edge with their beliefs."

"I understand what you are saying, Annie, but when a President is trying to bring about a change that would protect innocent lives, don't you think those dissenters are doing more harm than good?"

"I do but sometimes those in opposition get desperate."

"That's it Annie. This guy I heard about today is desperate—using George Washington as his calling card."

"What?"

"Between you and me the rumor is some guy is threatening her because he thinks he was our first President. He thinks President Romero has brought disgrace to the office that he set the standards for. He feels it's his duty as the Father of this Country to end her Presidency in this city—the first capitol of our nation—where he held office. Can you imagine! There's a sicko out there who thinks he's George Washington! It gives me chills to think he could be wandering around in those crowds. We couldn't stand another Dallas, Annie. This country couldn't go through that again."

"The President is well protected, Gregory. Security in the '60's does not compare to the standards now. The Secret Service encounters threats every day that we never hear about. President Romero is in good hands."

"I knew I'd feel better if I called you. I'll let you finish your work Annie. I can't wait to read the paper."

"It will be something. Believe me. Talk to you later."

The word sicko kept playing over and over in her mind. A gnawing feeling overtook Annie who'd moved over to Carmen's space. She'd never paid attention to his post-it-notes all over the place or photos taped to the plexiglass. As the clock approached 2:45 she decided she should. Looking around, Carmen's space wasn't any different from any of the other cubicles. Piles of papers and magazines and reporters' notepads mingled with empty coffee cups and a desk calendar still on last October. She looked closer. Underneath one particular pile were books; each with pages earmarked in different color stock. Moving the pile aside she felt the life drained right out of her. Staring at her was George Washington on every one of those covers. She told herself not to assume anything. She reminded herself the role history played in Carmen's immediate family. He was always quoting Washington. That didn't mean he'd gone off the deep end. Opening one book in particular she began checking out the worn pages. With paragraphs underlined it was apparent the book had been studied. As she turned to Pg. 74, a sickening feeling overtook her. There, ripped into shreds, was a copy of President Romero taking the oath of office. She knew the photo. It'd been an AP wire photo—in all the papers across the country. In black marker was circled a quote from Washington—*I walk on untrodden ground. There is scarcely any part of my conduct which may not hereafter be drawn into precedent.* Annie read it over and over, noting the word hereafter was underlined. Then she remembered the last thing Carmen said to her, *"They won't be able to miss this. Morris won't be burying this one on some inside page. It's one for the history books."*

That's it, Annie thought. Carmen's going to write his own history. That's why he came to Philadelphia. She had to find what he'd finished writing earlier. She had to get into his computer. But it'd have to wait. Steve Morris was summoning her.

"Press room wants it now."

"Did you bother to read it?"

"Jack gave it the okay. That's good enough for me. Send me the story."

"I already did."

"Gramps gave me the headline. Your story will be the front page. With sidebars and photos, Jackie will be damn pleased with copies sold on this one!" Looking at the clock Steve realized he was over deadline. "He'll be calling. 3:30's pretty damn late."

Somehow he was sober enough for the task at hand.

Back at her desk, Annie shouted, "Is it ready to go?"

"Just about. Why?"

"I have to make a minor change."

"Damn you. This has to go—now!"

"It'll take a second. It's my byline," Annie argued now back in his office. "Move aside before Jack calls. He'd want this story right."

"You are a feisty one," Morris laughed. "God it's hot in here."

Stripping off his suit coat, he then unbuttoned his shirt. "How about I keep on stripping? Damn Catalano. There's a mystery about you that I can't figure out."

Standing behind Annie, he moved his fingers through her hair, rubbing the back of her neck as Annie worked frantically at the computer. Bending down, he began nibbling at her shoulders.

"I'm going to make a mistake. Back off!" Annie pulled his hands away as the phone rang. The pressroom was demanding that page.

"Uh-oh! Little Orphan Annie can't come out to play. This little finger went to market—and this little finger had none." He was trying to distract her. That's when his eyes focused on the screen.

"What to hell are you doing? Starting a new story?"

"I told you I had a quick change."

"Looks like you've deleted more than you've changed. What to hell are you up to? Send it—now!" He went for the button.

"Get away. This is my story."

"This is my paper. You don't call the shots. I am a Morris."

Pushing the chair back, Annie stood and turned.

"This is my story—my time to tell the truth."

Staring at the drunk teetering, with his shirt wide open, she saw it—hanging around his neck instead of from the visor in that shiny black car. Glittering, with its cold oval insignia, that silver token was like a gun pointing to her heart. Annie knew that was the same silver chain. She'd never forget it, hanging, swaying in that night's horror. It was all in front of her—that chain, that obnoxious, disgusting laugh and stench of cigar that surrounded him. It all came thundering towards Annie like those ice pellets gnawing at her skin. This was the driver. This was the murderer of her child. From the depths of her womb she knew he was driving that car on old Co. Rt. 68. Months of anguish came gushing out as he again made a move to the computer.

"Nobody talks to a Morris like that," he ranted, shoving Annie back against the wall. "We don't print truth. No one pays for truth."

"You're a vile man who's forgotten what truth is. No one believes anything you print. They see beyond your sleazy headlines. They know Morris Publications is going down. The Jewel of Publishing has tarnished itself. Those headlines spell desperation."

"I'll show you who's desperate." He sat, ready to adjust the page.

"I told you. That's my story—and my story tells the truth."

Images of that night empowered Annie. Pushing the chair with that disgusting man still in it against the wall, Annie went to finalize the page.

That's when he came lunging at her, wrapping his arm around her neck, pulling Annie out of the chair and throwing her down on the floor.

"You've been asking for this. This will quiet you down. Put you in your place."

Dazed, her head aching, Annie couldn't move quickly enough. Oh how he smelled. That cigar mixed with alcohol smothered her. As he tried making his move, Annie heard Jacob whispering to her—telling her how much he loved her; telling her God was beside her and He would be her strength. That's all she needed. A guttural moan came up and out of Annie. Pulling her arms from his hold, she began striking him anywhere and anyhow she could—screaming how he'd killed her child, spitting at him, biting him, clawing at his face with her nails. Probably because of the liquor he'd downed he couldn't keep hold of this woman now rolling out from under him. She began kicking him while all along telling him it was for her child that she was printing the truth; her child he'd left dead that night in November. She threw anything she could at him—anything to stop him from stopping her. With him lying there lifeless, blood oozing onto the floor, Annie felt confident she could get back to the story. Leaving the headline alone, Annie replaced the copy with the truth she'd screamed about; then sent a story downstairs that would contradict everything the Morris Group stood for including the NGL.

"Print it," she told the foreman. "Jack wants it out as soon as it comes off the press."

She knew they'd never notice the change. The paper was already late.

As thoughts of Jacob soaking wet and in God's arms lingered, she remembered Carmen and her need to get into his computer.

Running back into the newsroom, she sat down at his desk. Everyone had left except for the cleaning staff getting onto the elevator. Deciding to call Tommy for assistance, she reached for her cell phone. A hand caked in dried blood stopped her. That hand pulled her off the chair and dragged her back into his office. Panting, obviously wounded, Steve Morris pulled Annie up and slammed her against the wall. Shoving his arm against her neck, he started choking her.

"So you're the one I saw whining, holding on to that dead kid. I knew there was something about you. Time to join your little brat. I have work that needs to be done."

Annie knew God had not abandoned her. His power overwhelmed Morris desperate to do Annie in.

"You're too late," she screamed, biting and clawing her way from his grasp. "The truth is being printed."

Shoving him back, he fell, hitting his head on the corner of the desk. This time she had no doubt he was either dead or seriously injured. She didn't wait around to find out. She had to get a hold of Tommy.

"I don't have time to explain," she blurted out, waking him from a sound sleep.

And so, step by step, Tommy guided Annie into Carmen's computer. It really wasn't hard as they all had the same user name. It was getting into Carmen's psyche that took the time. And once in, it was finding how Carmen had saved what he'd written. So much had been saved dating back years. Keeping an eye on Morris' office, Annie searched through each item aware that the clock was ticking and once that paper hit the streets bedlam would saturate Philadelphia.

Bingo! There it was. Carmen George Washington Rossi had signed off at 4:57 to a feature dated for tomorrow's paper. There it was with his byline spelling out the assassination of President Isabel Romero by none other than George Washington himself. He called it, "an act of freedom—of the People—by the People—and for the People. Quoting Washington as he so often did, he declared, *It will be found unjust and unwise jealousy to deprive a man of his natural liberty upon the supposition he may abuse it.* He continued, *The Constitution is the guide which I will never abandon.* With more quotes than substance, he declared, "Washington's act this day in February in his city of Philadelphia an act that would be like a gunshot heard around the world." He concluded by saying, "Washington died by his own taking—feeling he'd left the country secure in its freedoms and liberties as spelled out in the Bill of Rights."

Annie realized Carmen was not only out to kill the President, but himself as well.

Printing off what he'd written; then deleting it, Annie turned the computer off. Pushing in his chair, she took a quick glance around. Steve Morris remained still. Annie could only imagine the scene about to take place in this newsroom. She knew Annie Catalano would not be a part of it as Annie Catalano would be the reason for it. Selecting the elevator's down button, she was quickly passing through the lobby while stragglers for the next shift were coming in. Stepping briefly into the ladies' room, Annie assessed her injuries and freshened up the best she could. At exactly 5:18 a.m. as the paper telling the truth was hitting the streets, Annie walked out of Morris Publishing for the last time in search of the first President of the United States

Carmen's Place

IT DIDN'T MATTER IF IT WAS still early morning. Philadelphia was bursting with people. With her head down Annie walked briskly past shops and banks and apartment complexes. Standing on a corner in wait of a taxi, she watched as a Morris delivery truck stopped in front of a diner open for business. Out jumped the driver. Minutes later she saw him carry a few bundles inside. Down the block from there, he filled honor boxes and left more papers in front of a deli. Truth would be read over coffee; devoured as bagels disappeared and as President Romero prepared to take her case to the People.

Annie's first stop was the hospital. She knew the gift shop opened at 6. It was time to shed the heels and suit. It was time to rid herself of the make-up and let Annie Finley take over. No one had to tell her what Jack Morris' reaction would be to her brazen action at their expense. Catalano would be hunted down on the streets of Philly. They'd invent stories about her and splash them across the front page. But Annie knew, as the People would come to realize, Morris Publishing's tactics and ties with the NGL had been exposed. Once truth takes hold, you can't go back even by claiming Freedom of the Press for with freedom comes responsibility. The Jewel of Publishing was going down—faster than predicted.

Pauline wasn't in yet. Walking by the magazine racks, copies of the day's paper caught her attention. Looking at that front page, no one would realize that the story under the headline, "Romero Out to Kill the 2nd Amendment" actually supported the President. Romero wasn't depicted as a radical gun hater. Her story was told through the eyes of another mother who'd lost a child. Reasons and facts were given why the Amendment should be overturned. Numbers in sidebars revealed the truth—too many were being killed or maimed by legal and illegal guns; too many guns were finding their way from the States into Mexico. The last paragraph brought in the NGL; their tactics; the massive amount of money spent to buy favorable legislation and their ties to Morris Publishing. Annie left out the fact Susan Morris was bedding down with the Director. She had a feeling that might soon change too. All considered, it was a powerful presentation—most worthy of a Pulitzer.

It didn't take long and Annie Finley—bonnet and all—was walking about the gift shop. After leaving Pauline a note, she bought a paper and headed upstairs. She needed to tell Daniel about Steve Morris. News like that could not be told over a phone to a father who'd lost his only child.

Daniel surprised Annie. He was sitting by the window. Although still in a hospital gown it was evident he was strong enough to return to his farmland. His release was set for tomorrow. Sitting together on the side of the bed, Annie told him who'd murdered their child. She didn't go into any detail of her battle with Steve Morris. Rather she calmly stated she'd dealt with him—explaining her bruises came from falling while wearing high heels. She told him about her talk with the President. She briefly touched on Carmen. She didn't feel the need to go into detail. She confided in Daniel that her instinct told her there was still a story behind those scribbles and maps she'd discovered in Jack Morris' home. It was a story that needed to be told once the details were revealed.

Leaving Daniel the paper, Annie told him she'd have her cell with her. She kissed him tenderly, telling him how much she loved him and that she'd be there in the morning for their journey home.

Annie found the city wide awake once back outside. Surprised how awkward she felt wearing traditional clothing, Annie found hailing a cab a bit harder. Cabbies seemed to ignore her. But once successful, she took out her cell and called Tommy—drawing glances from the driver.

Tommy picked right up.

"I've been worried; same with Heather and Alicen. We've all read your story. How did you pull that off Annie? It's all over the cable. The wire's picked it up. I'm glued to the TV. Philadelphia is in an uproar between pro and anti-gun demonstrators."

Annie didn't go into details. Her focus was Carmen. Once Tommy heard about George Washington, Carmen became his focus too.

"I know he's not at the paper. He'd been given clearance to the Park—actually to all of Independence Hall because of his historical knowledge of the entire area. Between that clearance and a Press Pass, he could be anywhere. He could still be at his apartment. That might be the place to start."

"I'll meet you there. You can't go in alone."

Annie agreed. Tommy was on his way.

As if both cab drivers coordinated a time, the two arrived simultaneously. Remarking about her dress, realizing Annie Catalano could no longer exist, Tommy added, "I brought you a bagel and some juice. I'm sure you haven't bothered to eat."

Tommy read her like a book. Annie devoured the bagel. The juice felt good on her throat still sore from Morris' grasp.

"I've tried Carmen on his cell but he is not answering."

"Would you answer if you were trying to rewrite history Annie?"

"Good point."

Checking the mailboxes at the front entrance, C.G. Rossi could be found in Apt. 6.

"Strange there's no security. Must be it's between shifts. Hurry. Let's take the stairs."

Annie found her hips aching as they reached Carmen's floor. She had to put her encounter with Steve Morris out of her mind for now.

"Here it is."

Tommy knocked on the door. To their surprise the door was ajar.

Looking at Annie, he motioned for her to follow.

"Hey Carmen. Carmen. It's Annie—and Tommy. Hey. Are you awake?"

No one answered as further into the apartment they went. Tommy motioned to Annie to stay back.

"Carmen. You in there? It's Tommy."

"He's not here. Look." Annie was pointing to a note left for the cleaning woman. Beside the note was a $50. bill for her services.

"What's it say?"

"Should I open it?"

"Open it Annie."

Ripping the envelope, they read his message short and to the point, "I'll be away for some time. Lock up when you leave."

"Why did he leave the place wide open?"

"When you are obsessed you're not thinking rationally Tommy. Let's look around."

The obvious was everywhere—more and more books about George Washington and bookshelves stocked with histories. There were boxes of history books all over the place—even in his bedroom. In a side room was Carmen's desk overlooking the Square covered with notebooks and legal pads. Framed pictures of him with his parents lined one entire wall. They'd all been taken at historical sites across the country. The forced smiles were the same in each.

Sitting at Carmen's desk, Tommy began rummaging around. "How'd he ever keep track of anything?"

"I wouldn't talk Tommy."

"You're right. Creating brings chaos for sure."

"'In this case, chaos in one's mind could bring chaos on the streets. It saddens me so. Here is a family like the family Daniel and I had. We've lost our son. In some ways Carmen's parents have already lost theirs and they don't even realize it."

"They don't know their son Annie. They created a monster without even knowing it."

"How does that happen?"

"I'm not a parent but I think part of parenting is allowing a child to explore and discover who he is—and not who the parent would like the child to be."

"Very true."

"From what you've told me, that's how you and Daniel were raising Jacob. Despite stringent circumstances you were able to encourage Jacob to be curious. That's an extraordinary gift to give a child—especially one born into such rule."

"I still wonder what he would have done with his life."

"You'll probably always wonder Annie."

"You're right Tommy. But for the moment we have another young man to worry about. I'm calling Gregory. Alert the President to this situation."

Even before Annie could say a word over the phone, Gregory praised her for the front page story.

"We're so proud of you. President Romero has read it several times. How did you pull it off?"

"I beat them at their own game Gregory. I did learn quite a bit while employed by the Morris family."

"From what we hear, that family is hunting you down. Please stay safe."

"Annie Finley is back Gregory. My heels have been replaced by boots."

"Smart move. One more thing. Jack Morris is coming out with what he is calling, a *Special Edition* this morning. "To set the record straight," CNN said. This is a first Annie—two papers in one day. You really got them where it hurts."

"It's called printing the truth. Something they've never prescribed to." Annie could hear Jack Morris now. Ranting not only about what she'd done but the cost of newsprint for that 2nd edition.

Filling Gregory in on Carmen, Annie asked, "I'd like the President's permission for both Tommy and myself to be cleared for access to the Park. Annie Catalano's press pass is no longer valid."

Putting Annie on hold, Gregory returned shortly asking for Tommy's personal information for a background check. "The President has asked the Secret Service to make this a priority. You're cleared Annie. She asked that you go to the security gate. She'll have an answer waiting for you concerning Tommy. She also thanked you personally for what you did."

Arriving at the gate they were told Tommy was cleared to go anywhere in and out of the Park area. Both were fingerprinted and given security badges. Annie was asked to call if they saw anything out of the ordinary. Everyone was on watch for George Washington. Trouble was there were so many walking around dressed as any one of the former Presidents. Richard Nixon was a favorite.

Searching the Crowd

"Can you believe it? We are working on behalf of the President of the United States! And I thought I'd be at that Art Exhibit today."

"Do you need to be there Tommy?"

"I was there yesterday. They have it covered."

"I think I just saw one of Morris' trucks delivering papers. Let's see what they have to say."

With less than 2 hours before Isabel Romero would speak on a stage constructed under guidelines of a committee in front of Independence Hall, tensions were building. Looking into the masses not only was President Romero's photo attached to signs with a big, black X scratched through them, so was Annie Catalano's. Chants of *Catalano is a Traitor* could be heard. Camera crews from around the country were parked along the perimeter. Major networks had their anchors perched near the stage area—each trying to scoop the other.

"Good thing you're incognito Annie," remarked Tommy once they were inside a coffee shop. "These people are serious."

While Tommy read the article, Annie looked at its placement on the page. She most certainly had learned a lot in the last few months. Some of it she'd prefer to forget.

"That man is an out and out liar Annie. Says you had a meltdown; turned the place upside down; even threatened anyone who tried to stop you. Says you beat up on his grandson so badly that he's in intensive care. Morris warns people that Annie Catalano is out on the street—armed and dangerous."

"People know better Tommy. You can't distort the news on a daily basis without your tactics catching up with you. Freedom of the Press—like the 2nd Amendment—should be cherished; not misused for political gain or self-purpose. The Times Union will soon be like the dinosaur—extinct."

Once back outside, Annie started walking through throngs yelling obscenities against Annie Catalano. Tommy had a hard time keeping up until something coming down the street caused her to stop. It was an unbelievable sight; Amish women, walking arm in arm. Young, old; married, single, they walked as a community of one. They carried no signs; shouted no slogans. In the lead was Emily. As they approached, Annie stepped out of the crowd. Emily glanced her way and kept going. Then she stopped in disbelief. Walking over to Emily, Annie took her hand.

"I am still on God's journey. I want you to know Emily that I share your pain. I too lost a child. Jacob is the reason I shed my cloak and assumed the role of Annie Catalano. We are one Emily and when this is over we will remain friends."

"I trust you are in God's presence and your journey is His. I read what you wrote today Annie. Anyone who can write with such truth can only write with God in one's soul. I walk beside you—as do all these women from communities around the country who've lost family members to gun violence. Be careful my friend. We will pray for your safety."

Annie watched as the women in black cloaks passed her by. Some might have thought this was all orchestrated like a 4th of July parade but it wasn't. It was merely people tired of losing loved ones under the pretense of fundamental rights. More and more followed. There were thousands of ordinary people walking quietly. Many were holding photos of friends and loved ones killed or injured by guns. There were moms and dads; aunts, uncles, cousins, and siblings; teachers and doctors; nurses and clergy. There were motorcyclists and farmers; children and elderly; gays and straights all walking as one. Some in those treasured photos had been gunned down in schools; some in churches; some in the work place while others in their homes; some in their very beds. It was haunting to see the numbers. Mingled in that crowd were signs in support of Annie Catalano.

An announcement came over a loud speaker that the Vice-President would soon speak. Following the VP would be an interlude of music featuring Philadelphia's Fife & Drum Corps; then the much anticipated speech of President Romero.

"The best thing we can do is stay put. It'd be impossible to pick Carmen out in this mob."

"I agree Annie. This crowd is insane."

It became even crazier when Vice-President Parker stepped onto the stage. It was obvious his role was to set the mood; focusing on the human side of the President; touching on emotions of those who'd walked in her shoes.

"It's inexcusable in the most industrious; the most advanced country in the world that our children are being gunned down in our schools; in our streets; in our churches. It's time to begin the conversation. It's time to say no to special interest groups and focus the interest on the safety of the innocent. It's time to put the 2nd Amendment under the microscope of the 21st Century. That is a vow candidate Romero pledged. That is a vow now realized by President Isabel Romero."

The reaction was deafening. Emotions were raw. Over a bullhorn came instructions to *Repel Romero; Embrace the NGL.*

Somehow the thunderous sound of beating drums overpowered the bedlam.

From within Independence Hall out marched lines of drummers dressed in clothing of the era followed by fifers in step; their shrill notes cutting through the commotion. Musicians were coming from everywhere. Some were up on stage; others down in front. The door opened again. Out strolled children in costumes representing those who'd signed the famous documents akin to Independence Hall. The crowd loved it; screaming and waving as the young dignitaries took a bow and went back inside.

"It doesn't matter what side of the issue you're on. Patriotism belongs to everyone."

"Carmen would have said the very same thing Tommy."

The President's speech was moments away. Chairs were put in position for local dignitaries and politicians as well as the Governor. There'd be citizens representing loved ones murdered at the hands of illegal guns. There'd be honor guards from the State as well as the City of Philadelphia. The podium was secured. Flags representing the 13 Colonies lined the back. Drums began to roll. A young girl dressed as Betsy Ross was waiting to accompany President Romero to her seat. The introduction of the President would be by an Assembly woman whose husband and son were gunned down while shopping on Christmas Eve. Every detail had been meticulously planned. Thunderous applause rose as well as jeers from dissenters. News crews vied for position.

"I can't imagine this throng quieting down enough to hear what she has to say."

"Look Annie. Over there by that side door."

"They're just more Secret Service."

"No. I mean behind them. There are sharp shooters all over the place."

"Isn't that a good thing?"

"Sharp shooters are usually hidden—unless there's a situation to control."

That's when Annie's cell rang.

"Gregory! We're out in the middle of this crowd and...........Oh my God no! No!"

"What Annie? What's wrong?"

"What is wrong Annie?"

"I—I don't believe it Tommy."

"Annie!"

"The President has disappeared."

"Disappeared?"

"Yes. Gone!"

Vanished

THAT DRUM ROLL BROKE INTO DRUMMERS marching about the stage with fifers by their side. The musicians had received word to entertain the public as there'd be a delay with the President's appearance.

Chaos broke out inside Independence Hall. Uniformed police were blocking exits. Secret Service swarmed every inch of that building. Ambulances were on stand-by. The only problem was there was no President and no clue as to where she went. There had been no gun shots. No scuffles.

"She was seconds away from going on stage. She'd been held in a small room waiting to be escorted out of the Hall." Gregory had to catch his breath. He'd ran to meet them at the gate. "She was left alone for only seconds—seconds while the Secret Service cleared her way out and onto the stage. Some of the agents were standing right outside the door which was still ajar."

"Credentials please."

Again they were asked for I.D.

"You undercover?" an agent asked Annie.

"No. I'm a friend of the President. Is there any way we can help?"

Looking at Annie as if to say what in the world could an Amish woman possibly have to offer the most sophisticated undercover operation in existence, he simply replied, "No. The investigation is in the hands of professionals. I suggest you two leave the area."

Over a loud speaker the thousands in attendance were told again there'd be a delay in the President's appearance. The media was stirring; sensing something had gone wrong.

"We can't leave. We have to help find her."

"He's right Annie," agreed Tommy. "We can't do anything more than what they are doing."

"I remember once when I lost Jacob one hot, June afternoon. I'd brought him with me out to where Daniel was cutting hay. Preoccupied by thinking I should have brought more cold water, by the time I reached Daniel—Jacob was nowhere to be seen."

"Annie. They're motioning for us to leave."

Ignoring Tommy, Annie continued. "At first I panicked. It wasn't until I calmed down that anything made sense."

Camera crews were closing in. Helicopters were flying above.

"Once I retraced my steps, I knew exactly where Jacob was. We'd passed by a newborn colt in the field. Sure enough he was sitting right next to it. That colt grew up to be his." Annie looked off into the distance as if putting pieces of this puzzle together.

"You have to leave Miss."

"No. I'm staying."

"I understand your concern. I'm sure there's a logical explanation for what has happened."

"Yes there is."

"What are you saying?"

"I am saying I know what happened to President Romero."

Maybe it was her confident manner; maybe the agent thought she was an accomplice or a woman a bit off her rocker—whatever his reason, the agent escorted the two of them plus Gregory inside Independence Hall to the room where Isabel Romero was last seen.

"McPherson! Why to hell are you bringing tourists in here? Get them out. We have a national disaster on our hands."

It was obvious the man yelling was in charge. He had all kinds of badges on his shirt.

Agent McPherson filled him in.

"Agent Scott would like to speak with you. He's giving you two minutes."

"I only need a few seconds. Thank you Agent McPherson."

Tommy and Gregory followed Annie.

"You're down to a minute." It was clear he was about to blow.

"You have to call in a historian of Independence Park."

"I don't have time for this. McPherson—get this lady out of here!"

"I believe the President was taken by someone using a tunnel underneath this building." Annie spoke in a calm and confident manner.

"Impossible. We searched those days ago. There's no way anyone could get through."

"You haven't searched all of them."

"What do you mean?"

"There were tunnels constructed for later use that were sealed off and abandoned. Some are known; some aren't."

"How do *you* know this?"

"Carmen told me Gregory."

"Makes sense to me sir." Agent McPherson was beginning to think this woman was on to something. "There's no other explanation."

"Get me the curator. Get me some historian who knows what to hell is underneath this place."

McPherson followed orders. In no time he was back with two women; the curator and her assistant, a published historian on the Park who backed Annie's claim. She stated one such tunnel traveled below them, and continued through the Park, leading to a subway exit outside the area's perimeter. But she had no clue as to where the point of entry was.

"We'll take it from here Miss." The lead agent was excusing Annie.

"I want to go with you."

"Too dangerous," he replied, assembling a team. "We don't know what we'll find."

"I believe God takes us where we are supposed to be. I am supposed to be here."

Scratching the top of his head, studying Annie, it was obvious he didn't know what to do with her. After all, he was responsible for the security of the leader of the free world. He had input from heads of intelligence agencies at his disposal. So why would he waste time he did not have on this simple Amish woman? What was it about her that gnawed at him?

"I'm going by my gut on this one. I'm not responsible for you. I call the shots. Stay out of the way. Your friends remain here."

"I prefer being responsible for myself."

"McPherson—get some flashlights. None of this gets to the press."

There was no time for Annie to say anything to Tommy or Gregory. The room was cleared but for four including Annie.

"Going on the premise of a hidden tunnel, there has to be a place within these walls that leads down to it; a false wall—a hidden door," spoke Scott. "Pan out and check every inch of this room. These old places were built with thick walls and all sorts of odd crevices."

Realizing the door was ajar when the President disappeared, Annie searched the area behind it. Bordered by a wood casing, the middle of that one wall was inset about five feet with a period mirror hanging off center. Annie stepped inside the inset, careful so as not to knock the mirror down. Running her hands around its perimeter, her fingers followed a seam she couldn't see. She noted the seam outlined only one side of the inset and then, only ran halfway up the area. Looking where it ended Annie noticed a faint disparity in wall color and again that seam—as if two parts were coming together. Maybe it was her imagination but bits of dust particles were at her feet. She needed to find some sort of a latch. Her eyes fell on the ornate design at the top of the casing. Having only glanced at it before, she now studied it as if there'd be an exam. Turns out there were 13 stars etched into the wood. The star in the middle was bigger—thicker. Without hesitation Annie reached up and pushed it. That section slowly opened. The first thing she noticed was cobwebs—or rather, the lack of them around the perimeter of the opening. It was evident they'd been cleared away. Peering into the darkness a faint outline of a stairway was apparent.

"Found it Sir! No cobwebs means this is the way they went. Would you like me to go first?"

Annie was already half way down the ladder before Scott answered.

"Wait at the bottom. You're not armed. You'd make a perfect target."

"That certainly is the truth," replied Annie.

The climb down wasn't far. Shining the light it was apparent—again for lack of cobwebs—which way to go.

"What's your name?"

"Annie, Agent Scott."

"You stay behind me. McPherson you're last in line. Keep watching behind us."

The tunnel was in fair shape considering it'd been neglected for years. Damp; musty with puddles of slimy water scattered about, it twisted its way in darkness. Annie heard the rats. She could only imagine what other creatures called this place home. Even though it was February, the temperature below Philly was probably warmer than out on the street. About fifty minutes into their search the tunnel seemed to widen a bit. Agent Scott asked everyone to be on the lookout for stairways.

"Feel your way," he ordered.

They crept along, staying close together. Reaching a turn in the tunnel, Scott flashed some light against the walls. "Over there," he pointed. "False alarm. It's a stairway but it's covered in cobwebs."

Exploring with their flashlights, they kept going.

"Look sir. Over there." Annie had the spotlight on what could be another set of stairs.

"I believe this is the way they went. Somebody was in such a hurry that they left the door slightly open."

This was a good thing for as they wedged their way inside, the old door in need of oil was silent.

The light of day was blinding. Walking into a room, it was apparent from the furnishings and décor that they were in yet another historical site.

"McPherson. When we reach that Y in the hallway you and Tyler take the left. Annie and I will go to the right. Any siting of the President—don't make a move. If you see anything out of the ordinary, I want immediate contact."

Annie didn't ask a single question of Agent Scott. She sensed he cared more than he'd been trained to show.

The farther they went the more it became apparent that they were in a museum focused on the dress of those living when the country was gaining its independence. One large room devoted to President Washington was particularly haunting. It wasn't the drawings and sketches of the man or personal items on display that were bothersome. Most haunting were the many rows of statues all in his liking—each dressed in various attire of his lifetime. A winding stairway was the room's focal point. Tucked behind the staircase was a door.

"Stand back Annie."

Agent Scott slowly pulled the door open. Although the lighting was poor it was obvious there was someone lying there, bound and gagged. Not waiting for an okay, Annie went to the assistance of Scott. Together they lifted this person out of the confined area. Turns out it was the museum's only security guard who was in good shape and after a few minutes, ready to talk.

"This guy looking like the rest of these statues came from nowhere. He grabbed me saying some gibberish like he's *really* George Washington. He surprised me so that I didn't have time to think."

"Did you see anyone else with him?"

"No sir. He was in here when I arrived this morning."

"What's upstairs?"

"The museum's in the middle of a make-over. We're not in the loop with the other sites since we're not in the Park area. We're not yet open to the public. Rooms up there are being made over to replicate Washington's living quarters."

Showing the guard his badge and telling him to stay put, Agent Scott led Annie up the stairs.

"You can stay with the guard," Scott told Annie as they reached the first platform before the stairs curved to the right.

"I prefer to follow through as planned."

"This guy's not dealing with a full deck you know?"

"Who amongst us is Agent Scott?"

"Guess you're right there," he replied as they reached the top of the stairway.

It was evident that the remodeling was just about complete. The stairs led into the parlor; off the parlor was a pantry which led to a small kitchen. They moved slowly. Scott kept his gun drawn at every turn. Once through the dining room they made their way down a small hallway. It led to a room which appeared to be an office in the making.

"Watch it!" Scott pulled Annie back.

"This room's wired. Be careful. Stay right behind me."

Lifting her long skirt up, Annie carefully stepped over a thin wire. She followed Agent Scott's every footstep. Passing by a desk and through an archway they went at a snail's pace into more of the office. Annie sensed they were about to come face to face with Carmen as the area was full of books and photos and Washington memoirs. But it wasn't Carmen they met. It was the President, sitting at the table with her hands tied and mouth gagged. Stacked high on the table were history books; books on the Constitution—the Bill of Rights—and George Washington himself.

Instinctively Annie went to free Isabel Romero. Scott held her back.

"The President's wired. Go near her and you'll set off the trigger. We'll all blow."

That's when a voice—stern and shrill came rolling up the stairway. It was directed right at Annie.

She knew that voice. But where was he?

"Come on super woman. Find me!"

His words kept after her.

"Must be that get up of yours Annie. Slows you down. Better hurry. My time is a tickin'—and so is yours."

Annie looked at Scott for guidance.

"He's downstairs. I'll alert McPherson and Tyler to the situation. You don't have to go Annie."

"You must stay with the President. God has led me here and God will stay by my side."

Reassuring President Romero, Annie turned and cautiously made her way back to the stairs. Aware that wires could be anywhere Annie took one step at a time; reaching the platform and then continuing down to the main floor. The security guard was nowhere to be seen.

"Come on Annie. Over here Annie. I'm right here. Find me Catalano."

It was obvious that Carmen was in with those rows and rows of statues. But where? Once at the doorway, Annie stood, unsure of her next move.

"Why the Amish outfit Annie? Come on in and meet my friends."

She decided to play his game; talking to him while trying to find him at the same time.

"It's a long story Carmen."

"You're good at writing long stories. Morris said you were the star of Catalano/Rossi."

"You know that liberal me, I don't like labels." Annie kept moving among the George lookalikes.

"Tell you a truth Annie, I don't like history." He sounded like a little boy confessing a big sin and waiting to receive his punishment.

"I wondered about that Carmen. You don't have to like it. You can find other things to interest you."

"Too late! Too late! My head is full of history. Now—let me rephrase my original statement. I'd rather make history."

"We all would like to make history Carmen. Make the world a better place."

"Now! Now! None of that preaching crap please. You don't get it!"

"Yes I do Carmen. I get you!" Annie was weaving around the statues; watching for wires and Carmen and trying to keep him calm. She felt the weight of the Presidency on her shoulders.

"No! No you don't. I am history! I know history. *July 4th, 1776*— The first printing of the Declaration of Independence done by Philadelphia printer John Dunlop known as the Dunlop Broadside. I have my personal copy sent to me by the President of the Continental Congress, John Hancock on *July 6th, 1776*." The more he recited data the more agitated he became. "*June 7, 1776*—Congress meeting here in Philadelphia receives Richard Henry Lee's resolution urging Congress to declare independence. *July 6, 1776*—The Pennsylvania Evening Post prints the first newspaper rendition of the Declaration of Independence. I know it all Annie. All of it. I knew Delaware was the first state to ratify the Constitution. I knew it all! I am history."

"I know you know it all."

"So why did Tommy beat me? Why did he embarrass me in front of dear Mother and Father?"

"He didn't beat you. He answered a question."

"Father told me he won."

"It's not always about winning Carmen."

"Oh it is to Father dearest. He thinks I am a loser. I am here today to show him I am not a loser."

Before Annie could come back with a reply, Carmen jumped on top of a counter in plain sight. In his hand he held the bomb's activator.

"As Washington said, 'It is better to be alone than in bad company.'"

"You're not alone Carmen. I consider you my friend."

"You my simpleton—you are an impostor."

"But I had reason to be."

"'Government is not reason; it is not eloquent; it is force. Like a fire, it is a dangerous servant and a fearful master.'"

"But I lost my only child."

"Don't your kind multiple like damn rabbits? Go have another— and another—and another!"

"You're judging me by a label." Annie was getting closer. Out of the corner of her eye she saw the other two agents waiting to make a move.

"How would you like to remember me?"

"I told you, I consider you a friend."

"'Friendship is a plant of slow growth and must undergo and withstand the shocks of adversity before it is entitled to the appellation.'"

"So you're saying I haven't earned your friendship?"

"I told you I consider you an impostor—unworthy of me. You lied. Everyone lies. Everyone but our first President. I am not a liar."

"Are you planning on going somewhere?"

"Why?"

"You asked how I would like to remember you." The agents were signaling for her to stop where she was.

"I shouldn't have asked. I already know the answer."

"What is it?"

"Let the whole damn world know that I am President George Washington. Born February 22, 1732 in Westmoreland, Virginia. I am the only President to have been unanimously elected for both my terms. I am the only President inaugurated in two cities."

Carmen was screaming now; unsteady—more deranged as he lifted his arms above his head with his eyes shut and screeching for all to hear, "This is for all who hold dear the Constitution and our Bill of Rights. *Liberty, when it begins to take root, is a plant of rapid growth.* Our freedom to bear arms is rooted in words written by those who formed this Union. This is for all who fought for and defend to this very damn day the 2nd Amendment. President Isabel Romero is a terrorist—a foreigner bent on turning our democracy into a dictatorship; bent on stripping us of our rights and liberties; bent on disarming not only our militias but our fundamental, God-given Declaration of Independence and Bill of Rights. Tell my father—this is for those damn history books. I leave him my mark on history. I, President George Washington, do declare the 2nd Amendment forever guaranteed in my country of the United States. My country. My country do you hear me Annie? My country!"

With those words, Carmen took a semi-automatic pistol from his pocket—put it in his mouth and pulled the trigger.

Annie's reaction was instantaneous. *Help me Jacob. Help Mommy Jacob* she thought as she dove for that activator now falling from Carmen's grip as what remained of him fell to the floor. It seemed the moment lasted forever. In that single lurch forward Annie knew she carried the weight of the world with her. Feeling it land in her hand she gently grabbed hold as she hit the floor rolling; ending up in the midst of other George Washingtons standing tall and proud.

"Stay still Annie. Stay right there. You did it. You did it."

The rest was a blur. From nowhere came a bomb squad. Outside the area was cleared as their vehicles were brought around front. By Annie's side waited Agent Scott as upstairs the President was in the hands of yet more experts. It seemed as if it took hours—but it didn't. When Agent Scott told Annie they'd been given the all clear, that's when what had just happened right in front of her took hold. Carmen was dead. The President, safe and under heavy security, was now being escorted back to Independence Hall.

"President Romero told me to tell you she'll never be able to repay you for what you've done Annie. She understands your desire to remain anonymous and that's the way it will be reported. She *is* going to give her speech. That too will be one for the history books."

"I should have been able to stop Carmen."

"When you're determined to write your own history you're even more determined to control the ending."

Helping Annie to her feet, Agent Scott waited while Annie took a moment to clean up and catch her breath. He then called for an escort for himself and Annie back to the Hall. Investigators and fellow agents had secured the scene and would go over every inch of the building. The Security Guard had been examined and released.

Crowds were beyond wild. Word that something had occurred concerning the President was like an electric current running through the throngs. If ever it was time for a President to take hold of the electorate this was it—a defining moment in history.

Reaching Independence Hall, Annie found Tommy and Gregory waiting for her. They didn't ask questions. They knew when their friend was ready to talk, they'd be there to listen.

Taking Agent Scott aside Annie told him she'd prefer to be just one of the crowd listening to the President. "I will be returning home with my husband tomorrow. You are a good man. May God keep you safe."

"You are one strong woman Annie Finley. God most certainly brought you to me today."

Minutes later Annie was in the midst of the roaring masses with Tommy on one side and Gregory on the other. Late afternoon shadows were spreading out amongst those who'd been waiting forever in the brisk cold air. Although they'd been lingering, they remained spirited. But it was a little different now. Realizing something had almost happened to this President who'd chosen this city as her choice to kick off her "Path to Democracy Tour", tensions had lessened. Perhaps it was because those with opposing views had spent time side by side; getting to know each other a little better. Perhaps they learned they shared a common love for the country Isabel Romero had been elected President. Whatever the reason, once President Romero finally made her appearance the People greeted her in one unifying voice. It was understood the issue at hand carried a variety of opinions and emotions but at least the conversation was beginning. There'd still be interest groups and political maneuverings but for this February moment in Philadelphia a white flag had been waved. From nowhere came candles passed from one to another. As shadows turned to darkness those thousands of tiny lights of hope warmed the winter's night. And when the President took a personal moment to thank those who'd made her visit to Philadelphia possible one name in particular drew a resounding hand of applause.

"There are those among us who dare to do the right thing no matter what the risk. They are few in number for to do so makes them and those they love vulnerable. Principals guide them. Defending principals calls them to action. With this in mind, I would like to personally thank Annie Catalano for her pursuit of both freedom of the press and truth in the written word."

"We too thank you Annie," spoke Tommy. "My life will never be the same without you."

The applause kept coming. Cheers for Annie Catalano vibrated around the very place where such freedoms began.

"You've got guts girl—and great legs too," added Gregory.

"I'll miss you both. I'll never be able to thank you for everything you've done for me."

"Friends take care of friends Annie. My place will always be your place."

"Thanks Tommy. And Daniel and I welcome you to ours."

Even after the President left the stage the people stayed put. Fireworks turned night into day; painting the snow in dazzling streaks.

Annie's thoughts turned to Jacob; remembering when they'd sit in the fields and watch the stars. *We're going home tomorrow my little one. Home to Bear and to you in our hearts. God is taking us back to the fields and pastures; back to what I know is home.*

Home

THE BISHOP HAD MADE ARRANGEMENTS FOR Annie and Daniel to travel back home by bus. The thought was a buggy would be too long of a journey for Daniel. Although his strength had returned there was no sense in overdoing it. Surprising to Annie was how hard it was saying good-bye to those she'd met. She stopped by the market in hopes of seeing Emily. Although she wasn't there Annie left a message with one of her family members. Annie knew she'd be seeing her again. On her way into the gift shop to see Pauline, Annie noted the front page headline of the Tribune, *Liberal President Out to Destroy Your Rights.* Scanning the article written by Susan Morris there was no mention of the kidnapping or Carmen's suicide. Nor was there any reference to the President's remarks concerning Annie Catalano or the feeling of togetherness in the crowd. The way it read it was of an entirely different event. From the looks of papers in the rack just a few had been sold. *You people don't get it* Annie thought. *It's just a matter of time.*

Pauline had tears in her eyes saying good-bye. When she asked Annie whether or not she'd be getting back to sewing her quilts Annie had to think. It seemed like another person other than Annie had been that talented seamstress. She had no answer for Pauline. Deep inside, she wondered if she knew that person anymore.

Daniel was packed and waiting. Release papers had been signed and aftercare explained.

"The doctor gives you a clean bill of health. Don't try to do everything in one day Daniel. And if you get tired, it's okay to take a rest."

Annie knew what Daniel was thinking for she was thinking it too. Spring was a few weeks away. That meant no break until November.

Once out of the hospital and in a cab, Annie had time to collect her thoughts. Something was eating at her but she hadn't had time to figure it out. As the driver took them by Society Hill, it clicked. She was leaving without tying up all the loose ends. She never did figure out what those scribbles and maps meant or why Ira's son was in Morris' home. Remembering what the President said about there being an investigation into how guns were getting from A to B she decided she'd best leave it alone. She'd have enough to handle going back to a home without Jacob.

It seemed only fitting that Annie's brother John would be the one picking them up at the bus terminal. After all he was the one who started Annie on her journey. The trip back was a quiet one for Annie and Daniel. Although nothing was said it was obvious the thought of Jacob was on both of their minds. They'd never yet had time to mourn their loss let alone come to grips with it.

Surprisingly to Annie, she found herself glad to see her brother. It really hadn't been that long yet in some ways it seemed like an eternity. He did most of the talking; filling Daniel in on what had been going on at their farm.

"I've tried keeping those stray cats out of the barn but every time I leave they get back in there. I saw the other day one is expecting."

"It happens this time of the year John. Having kittens around will be a good thing," Annie remarked.

"I got your sap buckets out Daniel. I've been hearing the run might start early this year."

Annie spoke up again. Looking over at Daniel she saw the tears in his eyes. Jacob used to love getting up early with his father and going to the sugar bush.

"Maybe we won't be doing that this year. I mean, we are just getting back and there is so much else that needs to be done."

160

"We will be tapping the maples," spoke Daniel. "It's more important this year than ever to keep the tradition going." Daniel took hold of Annie's hand. That was the last word spoken until reaching that stretch of road along old Co. Rt. 68.

"Slow down John. Please slow down." Daniel's voice was cracking.

Pulling off to the side of the road, John brought the buggy to a halt. Of course there was no trace of what had happened there. But it didn't make it any easier.

"Show me where you found Jacob, Annie."

Looking at John as if to ask do you mind, John nodded, quietly telling them to take their time. And so they did. Still hand in hand, they walked the field to the place where Annie found Jacob. She told Daniel how peaceful he looked sleeping in God's arms.

"There were no scratches or bruises Daniel. He was beautiful with his little curls still falling on his forehead."

"Show me where I was Annie. Tell me what you went through. Tell me everything."

Standing in the middle of the road, arm in arm, Annie went over that fateful night.

"This is where I found you Daniel. I didn't know what to do. You didn't answer. You were soaking wet and I thought I'd lost you. I couldn't find Jacob. I screamed for him but I couldn't find him. And when the horse began jerking I thought surely he'd roll on top of you. I had to move you over here Daniel. And that car—that car with its lights and its music and drunken Morris at the wheel—I thought he'd run us over. He came right at us Daniel. I had our baby in my arms and he laughed Daniel. He laughed at us."

It all came out right in the middle of the old country road. A mother and a father's grief came pouring out. Holding each other tightly, the two sobbed and mourned their great loss as black birds flew in search of their next meal.

"I let you and Jacob down Annie. You've taken care of everything. You even took care of Steve Morris himself."

"I've down nothing without you Daniel. You and Jacob have been my strength."

161

They stayed a little longer. Annie picked some early spring flowers still underneath patches of snow where Jacob lied. They were the only early flowers in the field.

John had started the woodstove in their home. His wife left freshly made bread and donuts and a pot of soup on the stove. She'd cleaned whatever needed touching up.

"Mother asked me to tell you to stop by when you're able Annie. She's been tending to Mary who's bedridden with child."

"But Mary's not that far along."

"Mother can tell you more."

Thanking John for taking care of the place, Daniel had him drop them at the dirt road leading into their farm. Together they walked quietly along the rows of trees where Jacob played hide 'n seek; across the small bridge spreading over the creek where Jacob loved sailing boats made of sticks and twigs.

"Remember when the three of us made our own boats and we raced them when the creek was high in spring? By the time the race was finished we were all soaking wet."

"And Jacob beat us Daniel and you spent the evening making him a trophy out of wood."

"How do we do this Annie? I know we are taught to accept. But how do we go on?"

"Together Daniel. We do it together."

Mary

ALMOST A WEEK HAD PASSED BEFORE Annie felt she was up to seeing her mother. She and Daniel were getting by. Unable to sleep some nights, Annie ended up in Jacob's bed with Bear. Daniel was putting all his energy into preparing for the crops. He didn't go near his wood shop. He told Annie he thought he'd probably give whatever was in it to John. There was one moment between them when it was wiser for Annie to drop the conversation than to pursue it. It took her by such surprise that after it was over she threw herself atop a horse and rode him in the back fields until evening. She didn't mean to upset Daniel by suggesting they go to the cemetery. From then on she left that discussion alone.

Telling her mother of Daniel's reaction she simply stated, "We each grieve in our own way."

Annie had so much she wanted to say to this woman. She knew most of it she'd never be able to tell anyone so she tried putting it out of her mind—but she couldn't. What conversation there was centered on Daniel.

She did make mention of Mary possibly having a miscarriage, explaining, "It's God's way."

"What does Mary's doctor say?"

"He tells her to stay off her feet as much as possible. The spotting might be her way of carrying the child. I tell her it's in God's hands."

Annie said nothing. She decided she'd go find out in the morning what was going on. She felt as if she was on another assignment.

For a change Annie slept all night. She awoke to Daniel bringing her coffee before going to the barn. When she told him about her going to Mary's he cautioned her.

"You have no proof of anything Annie."

"My gut tells me something is wrong."

"Are you that same person who was bent on printing the truth? I want you to be careful. I couldn't imagine my life without you Annie."

"Don't be afraid Daniel. We can't live in fear."

Getting up from the side of the bed, Daniel turned back around and kissed Annie gently on the lips. "Have patience with me. Sometimes when I'm working in the barn I think I hear Jacob laughing. Other times I see him running to you so fast that his hat goes flying."

Wrapping her arms around his neck, she said nothing. Sometimes there are no words.

After baking bread and starting dinner, Annie hitched up the horse and headed to Mary's. She told Daniel she'd be home mid-afternoon. With about four miles to go, an approaching vehicle at full speed startled the horse. Annie had all she could do to control him as one of Morris' black shiny vehicles sped by. Pulling off the road, Annie sat watching two more roar past her as if she was nonexistent.

Mary was doing dishes when Annie arrived. Although not even three months pregnant she was already showing; at least to a sister's discerning eye she was. Annie made her sit at the table while she finished the pots and pans.

"Mother told me the doctor said you were to be off your feet as much as possible."

"That's right."

"So why the dishes? Save them for someone else."

"You'd do the same Annie. I know you would. We were taught God has a plan. I feel this child is under God's providence."

"At least let me do some baking."

Mary didn't argue. As Annie sifted and stirred they talked. The reporter led the conversation.

"How do you do it all Mary?"

"It is my duty."

"I understand but a marriage is a union of two."

"Ira tells me not to question."

"Do those men still stop to talk to him in the barn?"

"Yes."

"Have you met any of them?"

"One came in for a glass of water."

"What did he look like?"

"I couldn't see. He wore sunglasses."

"Is that all you remember about him?"

"He was clean dressed; a crisp white shirt, black tie and black suit. He was neatly groomed."

"Do the same men come all the time?"

"My oh my. I feel like I've committed a crime."

"Nothing like that Mary. I guess from being in a city I'm curious about things. What about the older children? Are they a help to you? What about Jonas?"

"Being the oldest, Jonas isn't home much. Ira tells me he's sewing his oats. I pray he decides not to leave the community. As for the others, they help once they get home from school. Speaking of school, they'll be home soon."

"Then I'd better get cooking." Annie sensed Mary was getting uncomfortable. She didn't want to press her too hard. She certainly didn't want her mentioning the conversation to Ira.

For being in a hurry, Annie finished four loaves of bread, three pies and cookies and even cleaned up the kitchen before any of the children returned. She told Mary she'd see them the next time, having promised Daniel she'd be back to help him bring in wood. Annie fibbed a little— telling Mary Daniel's back was hurting him.

Sleuth in a Buggy

THEY HAD AN UNDERSTANDING. ANNIE WOULDN'T take any risks and Daniel wouldn't worry about her. Of course they each knew neither would happen but at least they were trying to carry on without Jacob. The calendar had finally turned to March. Much of the snow had melted, leaving Daniel itching to turn over the earth. The season of rebirth was near but both Daniel and Annie were still taking it a day at a time. They'd yet to make love. The thought of enjoying each other seemed almost a sin.

After her visit with Mary, Annie turned her own kitchen table into an office. Once when the Bishop stopped she rushed to hide all her notes. She'd pieced together those maps and scribbles so as he came busting through the door Annie threw it all into the cupboard. He hadn't changed; still gruff; still peering into her home as if she was up to something—which she was. He told Annie he was sorry he'd missed her in Philadelphia but that the staff had told him how faithful she'd been to her husband; spending most of the days by his side. Annie made a note to thank Pauline.

Not knowing what else to do with her cell phone, she'd brought it back with her. After deciding to put her detective hat on Annie dug the phone out and recharged it at the library. She'd called Heather asking if she'd be able to bring her a wireless laptop. Her friends had it there in two days. They also asked, as Pauline had, about her quilts. Again Annie had no answer. She tried explaining.

"I don't know where that person went. I don't even know who she is anymore."

"Give it time Annie," replied Heather. "It will become clear what you are supposed to do."

Besides the computer, Heather brought copies of the *Tribune*. Annie read each one. Noting the total lack of advertising, she concluded that was the reason for the big spread announcing their new Director of Advertising/Marketing. Wonder how Joe is dealing with that Annie thought as she read another announcement stating there would no longer be a daily edition—leaving just the Sunday and online version. The nail was getting deeper into the coffin.

Tapping in to what she'd learned, Annie decided there had to be clues somewhere of how those guns were being transferred. It was unfinished business that Annie now realized had to be put to rest. Sitting at the table she put all the pieces down on paper—the maps and scribbles; the Morris vehicles on the roadways; what the President told her about the investigation; what Mary told her about Ira and Jonas. She ripped a map of the United States from a National Geographic she'd hidden a long time ago. With a black marker, she drew a line from the Indian Reservation on the Canadian border about an hour north all the way through Philadelphia and ending on the southern border with Mexico. If such a sophisticated operation was going on why couldn't any of the border securities or police agencies—state and federal—figure out how they were being transferred? She concluded it had to be the obvious. She eliminated waterways and airways. All that was left were the country roads she travelled daily. One morning before 7, Annie went looking for the answer.

She started by waiting in a thicket down the road from Mary's with a clear view of who was coming and going. It wasn't long before Jonas walked down the back steps just as two buggies arrived; each carrying two young men. Standing and talking for a few minutes, they went into the barn. Mary could be seen sending the children off to school; then disappeared into the house for a full day of work. Annie guessed maybe an hour had passed before there was any movement from the barn. One young man sprinted to his buggy; dropping what Annie guessed were blankets in the backend of each buggy. Another lapse of time and then they all came out. Shortly after that, down the road they went in a single line. Making sure they were far enough ahead of her, Annie followed; hurrying by Mary who was back out on the porch with an armful of laundry. Ira was obviously nowhere to be seen.

Comfortable with her pace, Annie kept going. Two hours later and they were still going. She'd never been so far down this old road. After a sharp curve, the gravel road forked off in different directions. Reaching for her pad of paper and a pencil, Annie decided she'd best keep track of all the twists and turns so she could get back home. As she scribbled on the paper, it dawned on Annie that Jonas was following one of those routes mapped out on pages found in Jack Morris' study. Annie was certain. She'd studied them in detail and as his buggy veered off yet again Annie knew where he was going. It was marked by a bold black X on that map. Turns out the X represented a farm much bigger than Ira's with three large barns and several smaller outbuildings. Approaching the place, it looked like such farms did on Sunday mornings when communities gathered at a neighbor's for church services. Buggies were everywhere. It wasn't the time of year for a wedding nor was it a funeral. There were no signs of a barn raising so what was happening remained a mystery to Annie.

Finding a clump of poplar trees, Annie secured the horse and went to get a better look on foot. There were no women; just young men milling about near the center barn. As Jonas walked towards them, they all seemed to rally about him. Annie wasn't surprised. After all, he had been on Society Hill. Neither was she surprised when she heard a cell phone ringing and it was Jonas answering it.

Thankful the ground beneath her boots was not all mud and the day was void of rain or snow, Annie edged her way even closer. Turns out she timed it just right as more buggies came up the dirt road to the farm. Greeting each arrival, Jonas led the young men into the barn.

Knowing they were all inside, Annie crept around to the back of the barn where she chose one of the two windows to see what was going on. Even on her tiptoes she couldn't reach that height so she moved boards underneath it from a nearby pile of scraps. It worked. Taking off her bonnet, Annie Finley was suddenly Annie Catalano after the big scoop.

The windows were streaked in grime. Spitting on the glass she cleaned a little corner the best she could without being conspicuous. Because all the young men looked alike in their dark clothing and black hats, Annie had to strain to find Jonas. She should have used common sense. He was right in the thick of it appearing as if he was giving a speech; his arms going in all directions. Because the sun was moving in and out of rolling clouds, it was hard to see beyond the glare. But it was that glare that gave it all away. As Jonas pulled open the backend of one of the buggies, what he took out absorbed the rays; turning it into nothing short of a bolt of lightning. And if that bolt wasn't enough, he kept pulling more and more out until the barn floor was lined with what Annie could see were guns. All kinds of guns; so many guns and now not just from one buggy but from all the buggies brought inside. Oh my God Annie thought. That's it! That's why police agencies can't find the guns in transit. They're being transported by buggies. Who would suspect such a thing? Who'd ever stop an Amish buggy? They're invisible as they go about the day.

All the pieces fit. What a well-thought out scheme. The Amish community was suffering from fallen milk prices. Many families had been forced to move away. They had no problem with guns. They used them on a daily basis. Tapping young Amish men to carry the plan out was rather clever for, at a certain age, most were curious of the outside; most sought some sort of adventure before deciding to stay or leave their community.

The trafficking must be run like a relay team thought Annie; certain number of buggies going a certain part of the way and then transferring them to more buggies until they reach Pennsylvania. From there the true professionals take over.

Her heart was pounding as she jumped to the ground. She had to use her cell phone. She had to call Gregory. She had to get this information to the President. That was easier said than done for all the young men were now out in front of the barn. The buggies had been emptied and brought back outside; the door locked. Annie decided it'd be best if she went straight into the woods then over to the poplars. But as she turned to make her exit she came face to face with a little boy about Jacob's age—and his dog.

Fair-haired with freckles dotting his cheeks, he stood and stared. Annie did the same. She didn't know what to do. She certainly didn't want the dog to start barking or the child to start screaming so she stood and stared right back at him. Sniffing Annie's boots then legs, the dog seemed at ease, wagging his tail. Annie reached down and petted him. That's all the little boy needed. He started asking questions. Something Jacob would do.

"Why were you standing up there?"

"I was playing a game."

"What game?"

"I was counting how many men were in the barn."

"Can I play?"

"The game is over. Maybe next time."

"Where do you live?"

"Down the road."

"I live over there."

"I thought you did."

"Want to go see my house?"

"Not right now but I have something for you."

Reaching into her pocket, Annie pulled out two homemade oatmeal cookies. Unwrapping them, she shared with her little friend.

"What's your name?"

"Lucas."

"Lucas, I have to go. It was nice talking with you. I think I hear your mother calling you."

"I have to go too. Thank you for the cookie."

"You're welcome Lucas."

Annie watched until she saw both Lucas and his dog running up the front steps and into the house. Lingering behind the barn a little longer, Annie then climbed over a fence only to be stopped in her tracks by a little voice shouting good-bye. That's all it took. Down the steps ran the dog, barking all the way to where Annie had just stood. Around to the back of the barn came two of the young men. Discovering the wood piled up under the window they suspected someone had been spying on them. And from the way that dog was whining at the fence they assumed that someone had gone over it. They did the same.

By now, Annie was deep into the woods. But it was unfamiliar territory. She wasn't sure which way to go to reach her buggy but for the moment she was more intent on losing those pursuing her. Don't panic she told herself; deciding it'd be best to stay put until the danger passed. Finding a rambling pine with thick, healthy branches, Annie climbed to a point she was buried in the limbs. Positioning herself where she could crouch down into a ball, she readied for whoever might pass below. It didn't take long. They were right on her heels. *I feel your arms around me Jacob. I know you are with me.* Annie stayed still as they neared.

"If someone was watching, they're long gone by now."

"I bet nobody was behind the barn. Lucas plays there all the time."

A gunshot sounded off.

"There's Jonas. He wants us to get going."

"It's because of all those guns coming in tomorrow."

"Remember what he said—it'll be the biggest shipment coming in here before they head to Mexico."

"Let's go back. There's nobody around."

Annie waited a good half hour before she budged. It was another half hour before she found her horse. As she hitched him up to the buggy, others she'd seen with Jonas rode by not too far from her. They couldn't see her. With buggies empty, they had a lot on their minds.

With the sketch of how she'd gotten to where she was on the seat beside her, Annie let the horse know they had to hurry. It'd be dark soon. She didn't want Daniel to worry. Once secure in the fact she was alone on the road, she dug her phone out from beneath some blankets and called Gregory. Luckily he was still travelling with the President. Annie got right to the point, telling him every detail; emphasizing the size of tomorrow's expected shipment of weapons and giving explicit directions to the remote location. Annie told him if he needed a map, she'd left a copy with Tommy; to call him and he'd email it. Telling Annie to be careful, Gregory had to hang up. Isabel Romero was just finishing a speech in Boston and he wanted to get to her with Annie's information before a scheduled meeting with local dignitaries and politicians. Gregory did tell Annie the President's campaign to rethink the 2nd Amendment was gaining strength. He also told her that the bomb Carmen rigged was a fake and that Carmen's father suffered a heart attack two days after the suicide.

Annie made it home just as dusk was coming over the back fields. Daniel had supper waiting. Small talk was shared. Annie made no mention of where she'd been or where she was going in the early morning. She just told him another busy day was ahead. No need to worry him. She was doing what she had to do.

Showdown

ANNIE MADE SURE TO PACK EXTRA cookies just in case she came face to face with her friend Lucas. Aware of what could take place today, she prayed she wouldn't see him. Daniel had already headed for town before Annie started back down the road. She left him a short note, asking he start dinner as she might be late. Annie decided she'd again wait discreetly near Mary's. She had no doubt Jonas would be making his move right on time this morning.

Four of the younger children were coming up the back steps of the old farmhouse as Annie led the horse down the gully and into the thicket. Annie could tell they'd been out collecting eggs. Holding the door for them, Mary had another child hanging off her hip. Annie wished she could tell Mary that her world was about to take a drastic turn but she couldn't. Besides, Mary had more than enough to worry about. Annie guessed about fifteen minutes elapsed before those going to school were running up the dirt road; still dressed in winter wear and carrying lunch pails. Closing her eyes, Annie took a moment to clear her thoughts. Those in the city might head to a spa. Annie simply listened to the morning songs of robins and blue jays; smelled the promise of the earth waking up. The turning of wheels on gravel ended all that. She knew what that meant. Like clockwork, Jonas appeared and just as he'd done the day before, Jonas ushered the young men arriving into the barn.

This must be their first pep talk of the day Annie thought. A few more buggies arrived; a few more minutes went by before Jonas led them back outside. Into their buggies they went and in single file started plodding down the road.

Annie remembered the way; staying out of view of the others. It was one of those mid-March days where it hadn't decided if it would rain or snow. It didn't matter. The trafficking was already underway. Once she reached the final turn before going down the stretch of road leading to that farmhouse, Annie veered to the left at the fork; mindful it'd be unwise to use the same location as yesterday. She knew the road would come back around to where she was going. She'd seen the way mapped out on legal pads. Choosing a place even farther away, Annie secured the horse. Remembering her cell phone, Annie then jumped over a stream fed by melting snows from the mountains. Staying alert to every move and sound, Annie made her way back around to the farm. She knew that one particular barn would be heavily guarded, especially after yesterday so she chose to stay on the edge of the woods near a small barn used to store grain. It was out of the way. With so much going on elsewhere this would provide Annie the perfect cover. She didn't have to be looking inside that barn to know what was going on. She'd already seen enough.

While Jonas seemed to be giving orders, Annie found a spot where she felt safe. It wasn't too far from the farmhouse and there was no sign of Lucas or his dog. From what sun there was Annie figured it had to be a little after one. Turning her phone off, Annie settled in; watching as slowly more and more buggies arrived. Another hour passed and that number increased to a steady flow. But today was different. As the barn door opened it wasn't the buggies that were ushered inside. Rather it was the two sleek black cars with tinted windows roaring down the dirt road. Annie tried desperately to see who was in them but it was pointless. They were inside before she could stand. And still buggies came from all directions.

Annie was getting flustered. Had Gregory been able to pass on her information to the President? If no one came, how would she be able to stop this obviously massive shipment of illegal weapons? The young men were blatant with their display of weaponry; not bothering to keep them under wraps like yesterday's shipment but laying them all out on the ground in plain sight.

Annie felt like screaming. She knew they wouldn't be hanging out there much longer. The transfers were underway. One buggy would unload; another would load. The barn door kept opening and closing. Jonas kept running inside and out with his phone to his ear most of the time.

It had to be after three. Just because the first day of spring was near it didn't mean it stayed light into the evening. If something was going to happen it'd better be soon Annie thought. It'd better happen or I'll make it happen she decided.

The guns continued to be loaded. There were so many buggies that they all blended into one. As Annie shifted her weight to her other foot, those vehicles backed out of the barn. With their engines still running, the young men secured their buggies.

Oh my God they're leaving. They're getting away with it. Standing; about to run right in the center of the action, Annie was paralyzed by the sound of sirens and marked and unmarked cars coming out of nowhere. Helicopters hovered above as law enforcement surrounded the area. Grabbing as many weapons as possible, the young Amish men rushed inside the barn and bolted the door. Those inside the sleek black cars stayed put. A moment of silence was destroyed by gunfire. Loud, incessant rounds streamed out from inside that structure so fast and furious that it took on the look of a Hollywood production. But this was real and those who fell to the ground were dead. On both sides there were losses for both sides were well armed.

"Come out with your hands up." From above, the voice kept it up. "Come out now—while you can."

The only reply was a furious increase of gunfire and as it temporarily subsided the barking of a dog caught Annie's attention. To her horror, Annie caught a glimpse of Lucas, following his dog into harm's way. Tensions were so raw that Lucas went unnoticed. Annie had no choice. Bounding out from obscurity, she took after him as bullets flew in every direction. As she ran towards him a strange thing happened. She envisioned him as Jacob; running and playing chase with her as they often did. She didn't hear the hell around her; only the laughs and squeals from a happy little boy. When she came back to reality it was Lucas doing the laughing. *He thinks we're playing a game,* thought Annie. She had to catch him before he became another murder-by-gun statistic. She'd lost her child. She had to save this one. Faster—faster she ran. She knew Jacob was with her. That could be the only explanation why she or Lucas hadn't been hit. *Push me my child. Push me. Keep me going. You are my angel Jacob. Push me.* And Jacob did. Annie grabbed hold of Lucas and nothing could have made her let go. Down they went, rolling over and over; coming to a stop right by that big barn. Laying flat on top of the child, Annie kept her head down—and prayed. There was so much noise. Helicopters kept circling. Automatic weapons kept ripping flesh apart.

At first Annie couldn't figure out what it was. But once she realized it was a fire she again had no choice. Without saying a word to the little boy, Annie scooped him up and ran and ran; never stopping until she was behind the house where she hugged him even tighter. Annie's decision was a good one for as she held Lucas that barn became engulfed in flames. Black smoke and ammunition popping and the smell of sulfur permeated the air. If hell had an image on earth, this would be it. The barn door flew open. Some went fleeing; some were on fire; others came out shooting. Mass confusion took hold. Men were falling like bowling pins. In the midst of the bedlam those two shiny black cars—which had remained silent and somewhat out of the fray—went roaring out of view. One rammed into a maple; itself going up in flames. The other sped away.

With rounds of protective cover, one of the helicopters landed as more young men fell to their death or were burned beyond identity. Heavy smoke made it hard to breathe. Annie's eyes were watering as she stared in disbelief at those running out of the helicopter—one man in particular. It happened so fast. From that blazing inferno came Jonas. He wasn't running. He wasn't panicking. He'd taken off his coat and shirt and strapped ammunition across his chest. He had guns over both shoulders and was holding on to an automatic assault weapon. The barn was falling all around him; his army of young men whose minds had been poisoned by those greedily seeking power by any means lay dead at his feet. Yet he kept coming. Slow and determined and as he kept walking he raised that assault weapon and aimed it straight at that one man in particular who'd departed the copter.

"Stop Jonas. Put the guns down. It's over. It's finally over."

With Lucas still in her arms, Annie came out from hiding to witness what was taking place.

"You can't stop me. You never could. You're useless. You eat. You sleep. You keep having babies and you have nothing. I want more. I want it all."

"I followed in the footsteps of my father as he followed his with God beside him. This is wrong Jonas. Put the guns down. Guns are evil Jonas as are those who've lead you and all these poor young men astray. They've used you Jonas for their own selfish wants. Put the guns down—now."

Annie couldn't believe what she was witnessing. It was Ira. He was standing with Agent Scott and other law enforcement. It was Ira; whom she'd ridiculed; Ira whom she despised for marrying her sister.

"So you sold out to the cops? Sold your own son out."

"I sold out to no one. I was asked to help. I felt it was finally something good I could do. But I failed. I couldn't stop it. We couldn't even find the guns that my own son was moving right under my nose. Put the gun down Jonas. It is over."

"You're finally right about one thing—it is over!" He kept walking and as he walked methodically towards his father he started shooting.

But it was Agent Scott who stopped him with a single bullet to the chest. Before Jonas hit the ground agents were on top of him.

Ira too was on the ground. It was Annie who was at his side; Annie with a little boy and a dog. Words, Annie again realized, were useless. Words would come later. For now Ira was wounded and needed tending. Sometimes, she thought, we judge others without walking in their shoes.

A bullet had grazed Ira's left shoulder. Jonas lay dead. From somewhere ambulances appeared. Reassured that Ira would be fine, Annie stepped back as he was being treated.

"Lucas!" A frantic mother peered out from a door halfway opened in the farmhouse.

Understanding the fear in her voice, Annie left Ira's side and carried the boy to his mother.

"This is my friend," Lucas explained. "She gave me a cookie."

That reminded Annie. Digging into her pocket she pulled out what were cookies. Now they were crumbs. To Lucas it didn't matter.

"Thank you." Looking into Annie's eyes, that mother said it again. "Thank you."

"I understand," was all Annie could say, going back to see if she could be of help.

The fire seemed to be self-contained. The barn was only a shell for apparent reasons. No livestock or hay had been inside. Annie realized it could have been so much worse if all that weaponry had been inside the barn. Still, so many young men had been killed; so many injured.

"Annie."

It was Agent Scott.

"What are you doing here?" Annie asked.

"The President requested that I come. After the incident in the tunnel she felt it made sense that I was a part of this. She was right."

"I'm happy you came."

"I am too. If ever you want a job Annie, I could use someone with your skills."

"I'm going home Agent Scott. I haven't been there in a very long time. Before I go, please tell be about Ira's involvement with you."

"He's been with the team since the investigation began. We were aware—as was Ira—that Jonas met frequently with Steve Morris in Philadelphia. We were all looking elsewhere for the weapons and sadly, they were right in front of us. The President sends you her best and her thanks. She asked that you keep in touch."

It was spitting snow. Spring was getting its kinks out as Annie wrapped up in wool and headed home.

Back on Co. Rt. 68

It was as if the horse knew Annie was exhausted. He needed no prodding. Fickle March was showing its true self; the wind picking up; the rain and snow combining into a soggy mess. Annie kept her cell off. She didn't feel like talking to anyone but Daniel. Darkness came earlier than usual. It didn't matter. That horse was on instinct.

Reflecting on all that had taken place, Annie was oblivious to the oncoming vehicle behind her. There was so much to digest. Although she'd connected the dots, she now had to take care of what was between them. Thinking about Ira and that scene of the injured and dead, she still didn't notice when that car picked up speed and started to go around her. But it never left her side. Instead, that sleek black car with tinted windows moved closer to her and stayed there. If a vehicle had been approaching from the other direction it would have been forced off the road. Instead, it was Annie being edged into the ditch.

It happened so fast. With the sloppy mixture of snow and rain swirling at Annie, it was hard for her to get her bearings. She knew she was on Co. Rt. 68. She'd been so distracted that she hadn't noticed she was approaching the Ferguson Farm. It was the light from their barns lit up that brought Annie to a shocking reality—The Morrises were back! This time, they knew who was in that buggy. This time, that buggy was the reason for their return.

Annie was well aware she could not out run them. They had her cornered. She tried finding the shoulder of the road but the asphalt blended with the night. There was no moon so Annie was on her own. Again ice pellets were stinging her hands and face; again the wool became drenched. What leaves had survived winter seemed to be attacking her. She tried to figure out a plan but she couldn't. Holding on to the reins was all she could do. The horse sensed the danger and as that vehicle kept bumping the buggy, the horse panicked. With all her might she tried staying steady but it was just too much. Between the furor of nature and the contempt inside that vehicle, Annie lost her grip.

My God Jacob. Please stay with me. If God wants me to go Home I accept His will but I have to see your father. Please Jacob. Carry me to safety.

It was hell all over again. The horse buckled; rearing back and then up on its hind legs; taking Annie with him across the road and down an embankment into a field. The buggy broke loose, carrying Annie another fifty feet or so before rolling over and over; ending up on its side. The horse kept running like a frightened jack rabbit. Except for a distant train whistle and that incessant wind, all that could be heard was a wheel going around and around. Annie lay nearby; stunned and aching. She tried accessing her injuries without budging for fear they'd be standing above her with one of their precious guns aimed right at her. If she played dead, she thought maybe they'd leave her be. But she knew better than that. Annie was responsible for their kingdom falling—one edition at a time. Annie had foiled their smuggling ring. If Annie had any chance of surviving their wrath she had to get to her feet and fast. She tried listening; tried figuring out where they were but she couldn't. So she went for it. Praying for God to give her strength, she turned over on her side. With one frozen hand in place, Annie propped herself up to a sitting position. Realizing she seemed to be only bruised, she then forced herself up on her feet. Dizzy, nauseous, she grabbed hold of the wheel but not for long. Annie heard them coming. She heard their feet pounding through the gloom. *Run with me Jacob. Push me again my little one.* But this time there was no escaping. She was just too weak. Down she went face first in the mud and grime and twigs that dug into her hands and face. She tried to keep going; digging her feet into the earth she tried pushing herself into hiding but fate chose another path.

"I see a wheel!"

Annie heard the voices. She saw the flashlights approaching. She tried blending in with the shadows but it didn't work.

"There she is; crawling like a snake."

I love you Daniel. Please do not live in hate. Accept what is about to happen.

That's when she felt a hand grab her cloak and pull her through the muck. She tried fighting but it was useless. It only amused whoever it was.

"Still got some life in you? Not for long," he laughed.

"Bring her over here."

Annie knew that voice. Steve Morris was back to where he first wrought havoc. This time revenge was his calling card.

"Come on! We don't have all night." Morris was impatient.

"Stand up!" Kicking her in the side, he grabbed her hair and pulled her up.

Somehow Annie found the strength to remain standing. She wanted to look him in the eye. She wanted her face to remain in his twisted mind.

"This is for the Morris family," he proclaimed. "You performed a cardinal sin in crossing us. We brought you into the fold and you defied our trust; ruined our reputation. You have caused us a great loss."

"You caused me an even greater loss." Annie was defiant. If she was going to die in this desolate field, she would die proud to the end.

"I knew I was wrong in bringing you onboard." From the shadows came Susan Morris; barely visible in layers of rain gear yet obviously filled with hate and revenge and holding on to a pistol.

"When a Morris entrusts one to be part of their team, there are rules one must follow. And you, Annie Catalano, broke every one of them. You have caused my grandfather great pain. You have smeared the Morris name and brought such a great decline in advertising and circulation that we cannot recover."

"I didn't do that. You did it. Year after year you printed what you felt like printing Susan. You were never a newspaper group. You were but a smear campaign, trying to influence the public for your own good. I only shed light on such tactics. It was the people who came to their own conclusions. And don't tell me of your concern about your grandfather. You care only about yourself. I pity those children you bought to make you look like a caring person. God knows better."

"I worked my damn heart out. It was to be mine. All of it. Morris Publishing was to be all mine. I was to inherit the reins. I worked my way to the top. And you—you, you ruined me and all that my family stood for. It was to be mine. I was to be Editor-in Chief. Those two brats are lucky I saved them from a life of poverty."

"If standing for lies and innuendos is what you've strived for then I feel sorry for you. Poverty can teach perseverance; shed light on what matters. It can lead to hard work which can lead to success and a greater understanding of humanity. Such a lesson is not taught when one is born into privilege."

"You don't talk to me like that!" Approaching Annie, Susan Morris slapped her across the face. "Understand; you don't talk to me like that. I am a Morris. I have newspapers in my blood."

"It's a fact you were behind the gun trafficking. You and others involved will soon be behind bars. That could be the last headline those papers print."

"Not so fast Catalano." It was Steve Morris now. "You forget we have some pretty powerful lobbyists behind us. And don't you think they have influence where it counts."

"You also have a new President cracking down on those groups. Now that your smuggling ring has been foiled I would bet the NGL will play footsie with the President to try to save as much of the 2nd Amendment as possible. You and your family are on your own."

"Shoot the wretch." Steve Morris stepped back as Susan moved closer to Annie.

Brave, determined, Annie showed no signs of weakness.

I love you Daniel. I've loved you since I first saw you.

A peace came over her. With her eyes on Susan, Annie began

to recite out loud the Lord's Prayer. Distracted by such resolution, Susan didn't notice someone about to take hold of that gun. No one noticed. The moment was so intense that when that arm did reach out, everyone was taken by surprise.

"What to hell?" Susan's reaction came too late. The gun fell to the ground. It was Daniel, now wrestling Steve Morris—the man responsible for Jacob's death. Morris had no chance. Daniel knew who he was fighting. He'd heard his name spoken as he quietly made his approach. All the pain and guilt of not being there for his family came out in every punch. It was over before it really began. Steve Morris was no match to this father seeking justice. He fell down at Annie's feet.

"Not so fast little Amish couple." Susan had the gun again.

"Drop the gun Ms. Morris. Don't add murder to your list."

Looking up, Annie was shocked to see that Sheriff who'd ignored her three months earlier. Behind him were two deputies; one holding on to the thug who'd done Steve Morris' dirty work; the other handcuffing Morris himself.

"This time, we've got 'em Mrs. Finley. Are you okay?"

"This time I am Sheriff. What brought *you* here?"

"I was at that raid earlier. I saw how you saved that little boy. Made me think how you must have felt when you lost *your* little one. I was no help to you then but I'm here for you now. I wanted to make sure you got home safely."

"Thank you Sheriff."

After introducing Daniel to the Sheriff, Annie told him if he needed her for anything she'd be available. For now, she just wanted to get back home. As she was leaving, the deputy had Steve Morris on his feet. Although Daniel had given him a good beating, the man's arrogance was still apparent. "You missed a good thing Catalano." His disgusting laughter followed Annie as she and Daniel walked away. Daniel had found Annie's horse. He'd return for the buggy in the morning.

Going back down old Co. Rt. 68, Annie filled Daniel in on the day's events. Daniel told her not to feel guilty on how she'd perceived

Ira. "We're all guilty of judging people Annie. What matters is how the Lord will judge us."

By the time they made it home, Annie had fallen asleep on Daniel's shoulder. She never woke up 'til morning.

Visitors

A WEEK HAD PASSED SINCE THAT fateful day. Annie and Daniel were trying to get back into some kind of a routine but it'd been hard. They'd had so much company. Agent Scott stopped to tell Annie federal charges had been brought against both Steve and Susan Morris. Apparently Joe Morris had nothing to do with any of it. He was now working for an online newspaper somewhere out west. Morris Publications was up for sale. While Agent Scott was visiting, Daniel happened to come in from the fields. The two men started talking and never quit until after dinner. Dessert lasted past nine. Annie promised she'd email him. The agent again told Annie he could put her to work anytime.

"Just kidding Daniel," joked Scott on his way out the door. "I now understand what makes Annie tick. She has the best of both worlds."

Later while lying in bed, Annie tried to figure out what Scott meant about her having the best of both worlds. She'd been confused since returning from Philadelphia. Having been intent on putting those pieces together, she'd put Annie Finley on the back burner. While she realized she could never live day after day in that rat race, she also realized she could not return to who she was before Philadelphia. She wasn't the same person anymore and that had nothing to do with losing Jacob. The answer came the following morning with a knock at the door.

It was Heather; on her way to meet Alicen in Vermont. Their conversation eventually led to whether or not Annie would continue sewing her quilts.

"This decision kept me awake last night. I go to take out my fabrics and thread and something stops me."

"I think I have the answer Annie."

"What do you mean?"

"It's that obvious thing you always talk about. Sometimes we don't see the obvious when it's right in front of us."

"I knew I had to go to the newspaper. I knew what I had to do in regards to losing Jacob and finding out who was responsible."

"True. But I'm talking about you and you alone. It's not selfish to think of yourself. If you're happy, those around you are happy."

Annie took a minute. "That does change things. I've always taken care of others. The sewing was a natural part of my life as Annie Finley."

"Exactly, but now, since you've worn another hat—meaning Annie Catalano—you're confused. I bet you liked going to work."

"If I think about it I liked—I liked the writing the best. Not the heels or the make-up. This is who I am right here but there has to be more—a mixture of Annie Catalano and Annie Finley."

"As I told you, I have the answer."

With that Heather explained. "Because Annie Catalano had so many loyal readers and because her work continues to be praised by both professionals and the public, there have been several inquiries as to how to get in touch with Annie Catalano. Tommy—as Annie Catalano's cousin—has fielded endless such inquires and I, as your agent, have followed-up on the more serious ones. There's a major publishing house in New York anxious to sign you to a contract."

"What would I do? I don't understand."

"Write."

"Where?"

"Here; at your kitchen table."

"Write what?"

"They'd start off with a contract for 5 books—fiction or non-fiction. They love your style; have faith in your abilities. They'd also like to get you up online. You can blog; twitter. Do whatever you'd like. And once you fulfill their contract, there will be more. This is ideal Annie. You get the best of both worlds."

Annie agreed. A. Catalano would pursue the contract. She loved putting words on paper and having people read them. A. Finley knew her husband would be most supportive. He always had been. She wouldn't have to leave the fields nor the home Daniel built for her. She didn't have to sit in a cubicle. She didn't have to shove her feet into heels or pay a high price for a cup of coffee. This *would* be the best of both worlds.

A Robin's Snow

DESPITE HER DETERMINATION, ANNIE FOUND HER body had suffered blows both from being thrown from the buggy, then kicked and dragged by the hair. There'd been no more company since Heather stopped the day before yesterday. At Daniel's urging Annie stayed in bed a little longer this morning. Heather was to mail her the contract. Tommy's lawyer would go over it at no charge. He was thankful Annie Catalano ended the Morris dynasty.

Lying there, Annie listened to the world outside her window. She imagined those rushing around the streets of New York and Philadelphia. She often thought how everyone seemed to be in such a hurry. She wondered where they were going. She wondered if they knew themselves. Annie hadn't looked out the window yet. She'd stayed on Daniel's side once he got up and went to the barn. They'd yet to make love. She realized it was a matter of accepting God's will.

Just dozing off again, Annie was startled by Daniel rushing into their bedroom.

"You have to get up Annie. I'm sorry but you have to."

Annie hadn't heard Daniel so excited in such a long time. She was up and dressed and in the kitchen in minutes.

"What is it Daniel?"

"Put your cloak on. Close your eyes. I have to take you outside."

"You sound like Jacob when he found the baby rabbits."

Out the door, hand in hand they went.

"Ok. Open your eyes."

Standing in the middle of the side yard, Annie opened her eyes.

"What am I supposed to look at Daniel?" Nothing caught her attention.

"Look Annie. Look. It snowed."

"I see that Daniel. But it's almost spring. It won't last. It's half gone already."

"Remember last year at this time. Jacob came running in the house all excited because it'd snowed just like this."

"I remember Daniel and you told him that was a robin's snow."

"Yes Annie. And he said a robin's snow must come from heaven because God makes the robins. This snowfall is from Jacob, Annie. He is with the robins. He is with all God's creatures. He sent us this snowfall Annie. I know he did. He is telling us he *is* in God's hands. Ever since we lost him everyone has told me to accept the will of God; that Jacob is in God's hands. Deep down Annie, I could not accept without knowing. I had to know. Jacob was our son; our flesh and blood. Our baby; and now I do accept God's will. Jacob is speaking to us. Jacob is in everything God creates—the mountains, sunsets, flowers—everything Annie. Our Jacob is looking down on us telling us not to worry—not to be sad. We can go on knowing Jacob is safe and with us for eternity."

Whatever aches and pains Annie was feeling had just evaporated. As bits of snow fell and a slight wind from the north blew, Annie's heart was full of pride and love for this man standing in front of her. In his own way he'd accept the will of God. In his own way he'd turned the loss of his only child into a celebration of all God's creations.

"I love you Daniel Finley." Brushing his hair back out of his eyes as she often did with Jacob, Annie embraced her Daniel.

"And I love you Annie. If you feel strong enough I'd like to walk with you to Jacob's gravesite."

"You give me strength Daniel. I must get Bear. Then we will visit Jacob."

Hurrying inside and up the stairs Annie grabbed Bear. As she was heading back out through the kitchen she happened to look through the window to Jacob's birdfeeder. It was full of robins.

"I see you my little one. Thank you for talking to your daddy. Thank you for the robin's snow."

As Jacob's snow kept spitting, Annie and Daniel walked down the gravel path to old Co. Rt. 68. They spent the afternoon with Jacob. Sitting on a bench John had made under the apple tree, with Bear between them, they told Jacob about Philadelphia. Annie described the Liberty Bell and how she met the President. Daniel told his son he'd be tapping the maples and how he found kittens in the barn. He also told him he'd be starting up his wood shop soon.

"I'm going to make some bird feeders Annie. We can put them here in the apple tree."

"We'll make it a celebration Daniel. Jacob loved celebrating. Remember the evening we all marched around the house playing the instruments."

"And the time he insisted on having a birthday party for his horse."

An approaching buggy caught their attention. It was the Bishop. Aware that she and Daniel were going against tradition by visiting the cemetery, Annie stood to greet the old man. His words surprised both of them.

"Sit down. Sit down Annie. From what I understand, you should be quite sore."

Annie wondered if he'd heard. She didn't say a word.

"I've prayed for you both. Although we are taught to forgive, the loss of a child is the greatest test of our acceptance of God's will. I've come to accept that you—Annie Finley—walk in God's shadow not in the path of generations that have gone before you but in your own path—in your own way. You have proven you truly are a child of God. May God bless and keep you both."

Turning to leave, Annie poised a question. "If I may ask Bishop, would you say a prayer for Jacob and for all who lost their lives last week?"

"Let us join together."

With Bear in one hand, Annie held onto Daniel with the other as the Bishop prayed for Jacob's soul and for those who'd lost their lives in a "senseless tragedy. Greed and power may have been the catalyst, but God's love shall prevail."

As quietly as he came, the Bishop left Annie and Daniel with their boy.

"It's time to go home Daniel," spoke Annie.

And so they did. Walking back down the old country road with Bear between them and a robin's snow falling, Annie and Danny Finley were ready to go on together. The seasons were changing. The promise of hope was in the air.

BARBARA BRIGGS WARD is a writer living in Ogdensburg, NY. She is the author of the beloved Christmas trilogy featuring *The Reindeer Keeper*, Yahoo's Christmas Book Club's December, 2012 Book of the Month; *The Snowman Maker*, released October, 2013 and *The Candle Giver*, released October, 2015. Her short stories have appeared in the Chicken Soup for the Soul books, *Christmas Magic* and *Family Caregivers*, plus *Ladies' Home Journal*, *Highlights for Children* and *The Saturday Evening Post* online. Barbara has been featured at Target Book Festivals in Boston and NY and on Mountain Lake PBS. Barbara invites you to visit www.barbarabriggsward.com; on Facebook under The Reindeer Keeper; on LinkedIn under Barbara Ward.

CPSIA information can be obtained
at www.ICGtesting.com
Printed in the USA
BVOW08s1247220617
487554BV00002B/5/P